William O. Stoddard, Frank T. Merrill

Guert Ten Eyck

A Hero Story

William O. Stoddard, Frank T. Merrill

Guert Ten Eyck
A Hero Story

ISBN/EAN: 9783337194420

Printed in Europe, USA, Canada, Australia, Japan

Cover: Foto ©Andreas Hilbeck / pixelio.de

More available books at **www.hansebooks.com**

A HERO STORY

BY

W. O. STODDARD

Author of
"Chuck Purdy," "Gid Granger," "The Battle of New York,"
and others

Illustrations by F. T. Merrill

BOSTON
LOTHROP PUBLISHING COMPANY

CONTENTS.

Chap.		Page.
I.	The New York Teacup	3
II.	The Sharks in the Bay	21
III.	The Press-gang and the Noank	43
IV.	The Cruise of the Noank	64
V.	Dispatches from Boston	85
VI.	The News from Lexington	107
VII.	The Great Chief and Up-na-tan	127
VIII.	Guns and Men	148
IX.	The Scouting Party	171
X.	The Lost Battle	194
XI.	Cutting out the Noank	217
XII.	The Hero	238

LIST OF ILLUSTRATIONS.

Guert, Co-co and Up-na-tan . . . . **Frontis.**

"*We must all spin, Maud. I don't want to wear a yard of anything made in England*" . . . 29

"*Think of the heft of him,*" *said Guert* 51

Boom! boom! roared out the angry thunder of the Merlin 73

He was like Paul Revere, carrying committee dispatches 91

"*Guert, that was your father's gun*" 121

"*God bless the mothers of all the brave boys of America*" 143

Up-na-tan handed out bag after bag to Co-co . . . 153

"*Howe's fleet must be close at hand*" 185

"*General Cornwallis, shall we shoot these fellows?*" 211

GUERT TEN EYCK.

CHAPTER I.

THE NEW YORK TEACUP.

IT was a placid-looking pond. In shape it was long and irregular, but it was nearly two miles in circumference. Southeast of it, on pretty high ground, lay the Commons, or what some of the old Dutch settlers still called the Vlacte, or Flat. Along the westerly side of that, and up past King's Farm on the ridge, ran the splendid road known as Broadway, lined with villas and fine, country-like residences. Winding along at no great distance south of the big pond ran Bowery Lane, turning up northerly and following the estate lines until it changed into the Bloomingdale Road, and went out to the Harlem. East of Bowery Lane lay the East Ward, where the De Lanceys lived, and the Crugers, and no end of rich people; and away above the Commons and the pond were the North Ward and Montgomery Ward, but they were more country than city.

The great city, with its business and its commerce and most of its inhabitants, lived below the corner of Broadway and Bowery Lane, opposite St. Paul's churchyard. South of the Commons were the Dock Ward and the South Ward and most of the West Ward, and they contained over twenty thousand people in that year of 1774, if the slaves were to be counted.

The city of New York was growing great and rich, and Guert Ten Eyck was sitting in his boat, away out on the Fresh Water Pond, and was not thinking about that.

The few perch and pumpkin seeds that were scattered on the bottom of his boat did not speak loudly in praise of his fishing ground. He was evidently a fellow capable of pulling in much larger fish; for, without being what some people would have called good-looking, he was an exceedingly sturdy and muscular fourteen-year-old, of full height for his age. He was plainly but almost neatly dressed in butternut homespun. His brown hair curled a little closely, and his keen gray eyes had a kind of dancing light in them. That sort of boy is never contented to sit still at his fishing any length of time without bites. In fact, you can hardly expect him to be very still or contented anywhere, for he must and will be doing something.

Guert was discontentedly thinking, therefore, and

he was glancing all around the pond. As he looked northward, he could see nothing beyond the flags and bushes along the shore, but he knew that a creek ran out through them, and all the way across the island to the swampy border of the North River. When he looked south, however, he could see a new boathouse building near several others, and he exclaimed aloud:

"That's it. The reason the fish won't bite is, they're all fished out. There are too many folks coming after 'em all the while."

"Ugh!" came as if in reply from a deep, guttural voice near him. "So, so! Up-na-tan!"

Guert was not startled, exactly, for he knew he had been drifting and was now pretty near the only other boat out. He had not tried to anchor his own to fish, for the pond was deep. He could have run out fifty feet of line there, and everybody knew that in some places the pond was bottomless. Still, what he saw, as he twisted his head toward the speaker, did not make him feel any better, for Up-na-tan was pulling in a very large, fat bullhead.

"Yo, yo! Yo-oh!" chuckled and all but shouted another and very different voice, and an even larger bullhead came whirling up, and was thrown floundering into the bottom of the rude punt which held the successful fishermen.

Guert had now floated near enough to look in and see that this was by no means the beginning of their luck.

"I say, Co-co," he asked, "how is it that you can catch fish when nobody else can? You and Up-na-tan?"

"Who you call Co-co?" sharply demanded the almost weird-looking black man, who was sitting at one end of the punt. "Name Señor Alfonso, any day de fish bite. Call him Co-co some oder time. Yo, dar!"

Tall, sinewy, brawny, clad in ragged homespun shirt and trousers, barefooted, with a face as black as ink, but with woolly hair as white as the wool of a sheep, and with hands that suggested the talons of a condor, Co-co was indeed a remarkable figure. Even when he laughed, he was all the uglier for his white teeth. They were so good, but they were pointed. They had been filed. No man wishing a slave would have thought of buying Co-co after seeing him laugh.

"Did Up-na-tan catch as many as you did?" asked Guert. "What whoppers!"

"Up-na-tan great chief," remarked the fisherman at the other end of the boat.

"Fish know him. Know he own 'em. All fish come to Up-na-tan. Own pond. Own all island. Own city. So, so! Up-na-tan!"

A trifle taller than Co-co, but with straight, coarse black hair and a dark, coppery-bronze complexion, the deep leathery wrinkles of Up-na-tan's face ran across a curious web of tattooing. His high nose, prominent ears, thin lips and sloping forehead, with his sunken eyes, gave him a face that had in it as little beauty as Co-co's own.

"No, you don't," thoughtfully replied Guert. "I wish I knew how to fish. The Indians sold the whole island, long ago."

"No sell for Up-na-tan," sternly responded the red man. "He not dar. Not born here. Only other Indian sell. All dead, now. No sell island for Up-na-tan. He all alone. Other Man-hat-tan all gone. He own all himself."

There must have been a pretty strong element of fun in Guert, or he would not have poked any at so ferocious a subject as the gaunt Manhattan. He was standing up now, looking all the taller for being in so small a boat. He wore a battered straw hat, a dingy red calico shirt, but below the broad belt at his waist were fringed buckskin leggings and beaded moccasins that had not been made by any pale-faced tailor.

"Yes, they did; they sold it," said Guert tantalizingly. "Got a whole bushel of things for it. Sold the fish, too."

"Look!" said Up-na-tan, waving his hand in a circle. "All Man-hat-tan land. Dutch come, give bead, blanket, rum; 'teal it all. By and by redcoat come, not give anyt'ing; 'teal it all. All w'ite men cut land up; say own it. Not own it. Up-na-tan own it. Some day Mohawk come—Onondaga, Seneca,

Cayuga, Oneida, Tuscarora — kill all w'ite t'ief; give island back to Man-hat-tan. Up-na-tan help. Black man help " —

" Yo, yo ! " suddenly exclaimed Co-co. " Not say so much debbil. Not say 'bout brack man. Guert good feller. Nebber say a word. Up-na-tan got he chief in he head. Get heself kill dead, if he don't look out."

" 'Fraid he's got something else in his head," said Guert to himself. " I'll go ashore. Old pirate! Doesn't he look as if he really had been one of Captain Kidd's men? "

He took to his oars as he spoke, and before the tall savage sat down again, Guert had taken several vigorous pulls.

" Co-co's another savage," he remarked, as he tugged at his oars. " Never was a slave. Fought his way out of a slaver. Killed ever so many Spaniards. He's lived among the Mohawks, and so has Up-na-tan. Old scalpers ! Cut my head off as quick as look at me. But how they do hate the redcoats ! So do I, some. They'd hang Co-co and Up-na-tan both, though, if they heard them talk of a slave-rising and the Mohawks."

He and the two dangerous-looking fishermen were evidently not new acquaintances, and he seemed to know what might be commonly known, or rumored, of their history. From what he said there was nothing in it to make anybody wish to know them very well. They on their part may have been already satisfied with their day's luck, for before Guert was half-way to the shore they were pulling after him. They were not rowing, for each was working a broad-bladed paddle with a skill and power that was marvelous.

"Take all fish to Mom Van Boom," said Co-co. "Mebbe some dose Souf Sea debbil come ashore."

Up-na-tan replied, but not in a tongue to be understood by civilized people. Either of them could doubtless have conversed with an Iroquois, and perhaps with red men of other tribes, but what was to be made of talk which contained also English words, Dutch, Spanish, and to which Co-co added more than one rough exclamation which must have come all the way from Africa? The very filing of his sharkish teeth proved that he himself had done so; and not only their talk, but the expression of their faces indicated that both of them were just now excited and were thinking of some plot or errand of much more than ordinary interest.

Guert's boat reached the shore first, and, as he sprang out, leaving his despised perch and pumpkin-seeds behind him, he exclaimed:

"I wish mother had some fish, but it's no use. I'm going down to see what the Mohawks and Liberty Boys are doing about that tea."

Plainly as he was dressed, there was something in the very way he walked, and much more in his correctness of speech, which marked him out as a boy of pretty fair education.

"I don't care," was his next remark to himself, "Up-na-tan has as good a right to this land as King George has. I heard them say so at the Liberty meeting on the Common. I don't want any tea, and mother says she'll never drink another drop. Hurrah for the Liberty Boys!"

Whatever he meant by all that, there was, nevertheless, more than one tea-fight going on at that very hour of midday meals and luncheons.

One was just beginning in the ample dining-room of an elegant mansion just beyond the fork of Bowery Lane with the Bloomingdale Road. The long, highly-polished mahogany table was not set for a dinner, but at one end of it several ladies seemed about to seat themselves, and among the luncheon furniture before them was a steaming tea-urn of solid silver.

If they had been about to sit down they had not yet done so, and one of them, a prim, stern-looking, dark-faced woman, was putting all her considerable weight into the indignation with which she demanded:

"Sarah Murray, what does thee mean by putting this stuff before me? Does thee suppose I would drink it? I should think it would choke thee."

"No; it won't, Rachel Tarns," laughingly replied the lady of the house, with one jeweled hand on the faucet of the tea-urn. "You had better sit down.

It's the last tea you will get in this house. It came from the West Indies" —

"Does thee mean it never paid George his tax?" asked Rachel Tarns.

"Not a penny," exclaimed Mrs. Murray; and there was more light than usual in her fine but somewhat mocking hazel eyes, as she added: "There won't be any taxed tea in this house, but I mean to save some for treats. Sit down, Mrs. Ten Eyck" —

"Maud Wolcott, why art thou so red in the face?" exclaimed Rachel. But the answer came suddenly.

A slight, graceful, very pretty girl, of perhaps fifteen, had entered the dining-room with a haste and dash altogether out of rule. Her chip hat was swinging in her hand, and her light ripples of flaxen hair were down about her shoulders as she breathlessly reported:

"Aunt Murray, I walked all the way. I ran, too. They've found the tea. It's on board the *London*. The Liberty Boys and the committee say it sha'n't be landed. There are no men-of-war in the harbor, and they say there are not enough soldiers to protect the tea, unless they take it into the fort. There's going to be a battle. Oh! I wish I were a man."

"Mistress Murray," slowly remarked a dignified-looking woman, bridling angrily as she arose from the table, "it is time for me to go. It is time for me to go. No member of the De Lancey family can sit and listen to treason."

"Sit down, Jane," replied Mrs. Murray. "Drink your tea. We are as loyal as you are. What are they doing, Maud?"

"Such a crowd, Aunt Murray. Everybody's so excited. There's going to be a meeting on the Commons. The ship's out in the river, where they can't get at it. I hope they'll pitch it overboard, and I said so to Aleck Hamilton."

"Did you see my son?" asked Mrs. Ten Eyck. "He is down there."

"I didn't see Guert," said Maud, "but there are swarms of boys, and they are all getting clubs."

Miss De Lancey's eagerness to hear the news may have assisted Mrs. Murray's urgency in getting her seated again, but her aristocratic face was flushed, and she beat the floor with one foot while Maud replied to curious questions of all sorts. The remarks that were dropping thick and fast were by no means complimentary to either King George or his ministers, and extreme loyalism could not but perceive that there was peril to the crown and throne, if this sort of thing were to go on.

As for Maud, so young a girl was not expected to take a noon-tea with her elders, and she speedily disappeared, remarking to herself: "They will never land any in New London — not while Uncle Wolcott is governor. They won't in Boston, either. I wish these New York people were all Yankees."

She need not have wished them to be any more angrily stirred up concerning tea and taxes, nor any more defiant of George the Third, for all she had related of the excitement in the city fell short of the reality. Doubtless things had gone from bad to worse since she set out for the Murray Mansion with her news, for when Guert reached the corner of Wall and Broad Streets, he found that there had already been a kind of rebellion. It had not as yet called for a battle, and nobody had been hurt; but he heard a man say:

"Yes, sir; they are going to board the *London*. We'll teach King George how to make tea."

If there had been, up to that moment, anything doubtful or thoughtful about the manner of Guert Ten Eyck, it vanished as he heard that, and he exclaimed:

"I can get there first. I can reach the Albany pier before they can. Hurrah!"

There was probably something in knowing just where to go, but the general crowd of boys that he turned away from went marching down Broadway with an all but orderly procession of stalwart men.

"Those are Liberty Boys," Guert had remarked. "Why didn't they wait and get out the Mohawks? No time to paint and fix up, I s'pose. I'll get there."

He was running now, and he ran very well indeed, past the fine residences on Wall and Broad Streets and out through the narrow cross streets which led to the East River docks and basins.

His comparative slowness just after leaving the pond, however, had given an advantage to a pair of very fast walkers, taking a shorter cut, and the two lucky fishermen were already entering a low-built, tavern-like place, not far from the foot of a long wooden pier that jutted out into the water as if it were aiming at a three-masted merchantman, lying at anchor out in the stream. Over the door swung a sign with a rudely-painted, open-jawed shark's head.

Co-co and the Manhattan were walking right in, through a narrow entry in the middle of what might be called the Shark's Head Inn, when their way was barred by a woman who seemed to almost fill the passageway.

"Squaw get out of chief's way," growled the Indian haughtily; but Co-co only remarked:

"Mom Van Boom"—before he was cut off by sharp, decisive utterances of her own.

Translated from Dutch into English and illustrated by gesticulations, they meant:

"The redskin may go in, but that black fellow does not belong there. He can't go in."

Co-co's temper was showing itself in his face dangerously, but his friend put out one hand and pushed the landlady by the shoulder, while with the other he pointed at his comrade, and said:

"No Co-co. Señor Alfonso. So, so! Up-na-tan. Mom Van Boom get out of the way."

Almost anybody living would have done so, glancing in those two faces; but a gleam of intelligence shot across that of Mom Van Boom, and she stepped aside. As she did so, Co-co handed her a pretty heavy string of perch and bullheads, saying something in Dutch about what may have been a tavern score she had against him. She and her finny load went out of the entry through a door at the left, while her two unhandsome guests stalked on through the house, went across a small paved yard, and a door that was at once opened before them let them into a room which seemed to be dense with the smoke from many tobacco pipes.

Just as Co-co, if he were not to be feathered as Señor Alfonso, with Up-na-tan, disappeared through that low doorway, Guert Ten Eyck came springing like a young deer toward the Albany pier, exclaiming:

"I'll take any boat I can find. It isn't any time to pick and choose."

There was no picking and choosing for any man to do in that vicinity. It was not any kind of boating station. There was not even a vessel lying at that wharf, although others above were by no means unoccupied, and there was a large East Indiaman in the West Dock undergoing repairs.

The tide was running out, and it floated, at the end of a short hawser, a very serviceable-looking little craft that plainly did not belong to any ship.

"Hurrah!" shouted Guert, pulling it in, and

springing on board. "Steven De Lancey's *Petrel*. Wouldn't he be mad if he knew what she's going to do? Two pair of oars and a sail."

He did not put the sail up, but he had cast loose in a moment, and he showed right good muscle as well as skill in the way he sculled the *Petrel* out and across toward the West Dock.

"There go the Liberty Boys," he shouted. "I'll be there in time. They're going out after the tea."

While he was making the *Petrel*—the first prize captured in the long struggle against King George and his taxes—Up-na-tan and Co-co were talking, in other tongues than English, with a lot of men who were almost as remarkable as they were themselves. That is, they looked like seafaring men, picked out of the worst lots that could be found, all over the world. One of them was a Chinaman, and another looked like a Malay, and another may have been a South Sea Islander. It was hard to guess where all the rest of the baker's dozen came from; and what they might be there for was even a greater mystery. If there had been a British man-of-war in the harbor, short of seamen, it would have needed to send half its crew as a press-gang to capture the sailor guests of Mom Van Boom. They all carried sheath-knives openly, but only one of their number, seemingly of some authority, wore a sword. It was a "hanger," a cut-and-thrust weapon, half-way between a cutlass and a gentleman's dress sword.

Co-co was on his dignity, and, as if by common consent, they called him Señor, while they seemed to have an especial knowledge of, and respect for, "the chief," as they called the Manhattan. Not any ordinary chance listener could have gathered much information from the conversation, but it seemed to relate to some deeply interesting subject, if not to several subjects, such as might interest that kind, or those kinds of men.

Mom Van Boom was in her kitchen, preparing bullheads for the frying-pan, and she had hardly thrown in her first fish when Guert Ten Eyck, sculling the *Petrel* up to the wharf, was greeted with:

"Halloo, boy! We want that boat."

"That's what I brought her for, Mr. Verplanck," shouted Guert. "I want four oarsmen, though. We'll put the Liberty Boys right on board the *London*."

"You are one of them," responded, heartily, another voice. "We needed another boat."

"Here she is," said Guert; and he looked as if he had won a victory.

His brown-tanned face was all aglow; his eyes were jubilant, and so was his voice. He seemed a year older. He did not know how perfectly he was a representative of all the hearty, healthy boys of the land he belonged to; brimming with courage, intelligence and love of adventure, but ready, first of all, to take fire in opposition to anything like tyranny or oppression.

If he knew very little about the authority of the King and Parliament to levy taxes on the American colonies, he felt, by instinct, that he was in the right place, steering a boat for the grown-up patriots who were going to board the *London*. Stronger arms took possession of the oars, but Guert seated himself at the rudder, no one objecting, and the boat was instantly full of men. None of them were armed, apparently, but all wore looks of grim determination. There were three other boats, of different sizes, putting off at the same time; but orders shouted by some one in command kept them in company, and they all arrived together at the starboard side of the *London*. One man was left in each boat, but Guert was among the swarm that clambered over the low bulwarks of the vessel containing the tea that threatened the liberties of America.

Away up, beyond the Bowery Lane, a little luncheon party of ladies was just then breaking up with a deal of stiffness and formality, considering they were all old neighbors, who had known each other from childhood.

"It will be treason if they touch that tea," said Miss De Lancey. "How can a Quaker like Rachel Tarns favor rebellion?"

"Thee is wrong, Jane," said Rachel. "I counsel not the use of carnal weapons, nor resistance to authority, but I will not drink thy tea after it is taxed."

Barely was Miss De Lancey out of hearing before Maud Wolcott loudly whispered to the unpeacefullooking disciple of William Penn: "Rachel Tarns, I wouldn't say it while she was here — they are really going to pitch it all overboard."

"Thee is a good girl," said Rachel. "Thy people in Connecticut will not be partakers of the evil thing."

"Aunt Murray won't," said Maud, "nor any of the Wolcotts."

On board the *London* it began to look as if Maud might be correct. There was no loud talking, and there was no need for violence. Men went at once down into the hold, and a tackle was rigged down a hatchway.

"Ready?" asked the man at the tackle.

"Up!" shouted a voice below, and a fine green tea-chest came swinging up and was landed on the deck.

Down went the tackle-hooks for another, but Guert could not have restrained himself, if he had tried. He was at the side of that tea-chest like a flash, and it went end over end to the side of the vessel.

"Up!" again shouted the men below, but the word seemed also a command to a couple of stalwart patriots who had followed Guert. He did not have to lift the chest after he had knocked off its cover with a hand spike. It arose to the bulwark as if it did not weigh an ounce, and out went the fragrant China leaves into the salt water.

That was the last chest Guert could get hold of. One after another, more came up, however, until no less than eighteen had been opened and emptied.

"It's all there was on board," said Guert. "What a pity; I wish there had been a thousand. It's pretty weak tea."

He was looking into the water as he said that, but there was a general movement toward the boats, and it forced him to think of the *Petrel*.

"Steve De Lancey'll never know," he said, as he went down into her; "but if it's treason, his boat helped do it. I want to tell mother and Maud Wolcott."

He was not to tell the story of his wonderful afternoon to anybody up town, right away. His first landing was made quickly enough, and after the men were out of her he sculled the *Petrel* to the wharf where he had found her.

Two tall figures stood there, watching him as if waiting for him. No sooner did the boat's nose come within their reach than Up-na-tan first and then Co-co stepped on board, pushed her off with sudden vigor, and silently put up the sail. Guert was so astonished that for a moment he said nothing, but the first indignant protest he uttered was replied to by:

"Chief no hurt boy. Bring him back safe. Want boat. So, so! Up-na-tan."

"Whar you been?" asked Co-co somberly, and Guert was willing enough to tell them about the tea, while they steered the *Petrel* straight out for Buttermilk Channel, that led to the bay and the sea.

CHAPTER II.

THE SHARKS IN THE BAY.

THERE was a ringing of rapid horse-hoofs upon the graveled carriage-way leading up to the piazza of the Murray mansion.

The guests who had so nearly quarreled over the tea question had all departed, and they had all gone away on good terms with Mrs. Murray. She was a very bright, polite, hospitable little woman, with a rare tact for meeting all sorts of people, and for saying what she pleased to them without letting them get offended. That was why, perhaps, people on opposite sides could come to her house and talk at each other. So it was about the best visited house in all that neighborhood.

"Somebody's coming!" exclaimed Maud, hurrying out, and in a moment more Mrs. Murray herself greeted a horseman, who was dismounting at the foot of the steps, with:

"O, Steven! Your Aunt Jane has just gone home. Is there any more news? Tell me, quick!"

Maud Wolcott was just behind her, and added excitedly:

"Please, Mr. De Lancey! What did they do with the tea?"

He was a broad-shouldered, handsome young fellow, carefully well-dressed, and his somewhat haughty face was more than a little flushed, as he replied:

"I've raced all the way down from East Chester. Mounted and rode as soon as I heard that anything was up. The rebels! I stopped here to learn what I could" —

"O, dear!" exclaimed Mrs. Murray. "I hoped you could tell us something. All we know is" — and with Maud's help the young patrician quickly knew as much as they did, and perhaps more than they knew, with any certainty.

The young man heard with every token of well-bred deference, but he said:

"There should have been a regiment of the line there, or at least a company of troopers, to scatter those fellows. I'll ride on down, and find out what they did. It is time loyal men began to do something."

"Why, Mr. De Lancey!" exclaimed Maud, wonderingly. "You are not on the wrong side, are you? Isn't this your own country?"

De Lancey bowed low, for the enthusiastic young rebel was looking her very prettiest; but he was true to his principles, for he said:

"Yes; it is, Miss Wolcott. It is my country and my king's. I belong to the king. My ancestors have been the king's men since they rode behind William to conquer England. Every De Lancey will be found on the right side, if there is to be any trouble now."

"Oh! I hope there won't be," exclaimed Mrs. Murray. "Why, Steven, it would be dreadful. I'm as loyal as you are to the king. But then, his ministers" —

That gave Steven a chance to escape, for his face brightened, and he turned to his horse, saying:

"Now, Mrs. Murray, that's politics. I'm not in Parliament. I'll go."

Just as he was mounting, he could have heard Maud's sharp rejoinder:

"My uncle, Governor Wolcott of Connecticut, says that's the difficulty. They won't let Americans send anybody to Parliament. We are governed without our own consent."

De Lancey was in the saddle, with the ease and grace of a perfect horseman, and he only lifted and waved his hat, smiling at both the ladies, as he spurred hastily away to gallop down the Bowery Lane. He was on his way home, too, for his own family mansion looked out upon the East River, below the broad acres of the Stuyvesants.

"He would make a splendid captain of cavalry," muttered Mrs. Murray, as he disappeared. "The

De Lanceys were Cavaliers when the Murrays were Covenanters.''

Perhaps, therefore, the roots of the opposition to kingly rule went down deeper than the tea-tax question. So far, at least, as the New York Dutch were concerned, none of them could fairly be expected to feel like the De Lanceys. Neither could Indians, nor black people, nor Quakers, nor New England Puritans, such as the Wolcotts.

Maud herself had darted into the house, and she now came out with her hat on, exclaiming:

"Aunt Murray, please let me go over to Mrs. Ten Eyck's. Guert may have gotten home. He will know everything."

"Go, go!" eagerly responded Mrs. Murray. "Find what they did with the tea. I'm glad I've half a chest in the storeroom that didn't pay duty. Come right back."

Maud was already down the steps, and her hat on her head wrong side foremost.

"There are other men," she said to herself, "that will make as good soldiers as Steven De Lancey or any of them. I wish I could fight! I'll just see what Guert has to say."

He was having quite enough to say at that very moment. All his talk about the tea had long since ended, and his savage-looking friends had heard his account with strong expressions of approval. He had seemed to grow, before their very eyes, from a mere boy — for whose mother they had sometimes done farmwork, as appeared in the conversation — into a daring young rover, who had actually been in a boarding party and had helped capture a ship. It was a kind of service which appealed to them peculiarly, and they said so to each other in tongues that he did not understand. As for other talk, they greatly preferred Dutch, and Guert was at home in that.

His present burst of questions was prompted by the fact that the *Petrel* had already tacked her way through Buttermilk Channel. She was now below Governor's Island, and Co-co, at the tiller, was pointing her sharp nose right out into the broad New York Bay.

"Where are we going?" again and very earnestly demanded Guert.

"Yo, yo!" laughed Co-co. "Go ober sea. Talk King George 'bout tea-ship."

"No talk," said the Manhattan gloomily. "Up-na-tan head heap full. Hard think."

Guert was silent, for he, too, was thinking hard; and he did not at all like the look of things. The *Petrel* was a stanch boat, and they were prime seamen; but the breeze on the bay was fresh, and the little yacht was leaning over almost gunwale under, as she drove on into rougher and rougher water.

"The old pirate!" he said to himself. "Co-co's as bad as he is. He was an Ashantee warrior. Worst kind. Regular old cannibal. Wish he'd never come from Africa. Where on earth are they taking me? There's no fishing now done out here. Well, yes; there is. I wasn't thinking of bluefish."

The red man and his African mate had thought of it, however, for now a couple of lines, mounted with bone-squid hooks, were produced, and the crew of the *Petrel* had a good excuse to offer for being out in the Bay.

"Guert take line," said Up-na-tan. "No bullhead here. Catch heap."

There was a very strong impression on Guert's mind, he could not say why, that fishing was not by any means the real errand they were on. He felt dreadfully uneasy, too, about being with them in what was really a stolen boat, for the city laws concerning such things were cruelly severe. It was especially ordained that no black man should own such a boat as the *Petrel*, and that no black man, slave or free, should use one without especial permission or responsible white company. Indians were left more at liberty, for they were very few around New York; but then, Up-na-tan was the most suspicious character among them, and was liable to be strictly dealt with at any time. Most good citizens believed and declared that he ought to have been taken to Gibbet Island long ago.

Guert's thoughts, as he watched his squid twinkling in the wake of the boat, were suddenly interrupted by the vigorous "strike" of a bluefish, and in a second more he was pulling in with all his strength, for he had hooked a ten-pounder.

"Yo, yo!" shouted Co-co, as the Manhattan jerked his line and began to haul upon a heavier fish than Guert's.

"Up-na-tan own bay. Ugh!" responded the Indian. "Own heap bluefish. Own shark."

Guert saw little meaning in that remark for a minute or so; but just as he lifted his struggling prize, and triumphantly threw him down to flop on the bottom of the boat, a side-glance to leeward showed him a foamy flash on the crest of a wave. It was followed by a long black-and-white streak and a plunging leap, and he knew that he had seen the largest shark he had ever yet seen.

"Ugh!" said Up-na-tan; but a look of the most intense ferocity shot across the face of the Ashantee as he remarked:

"Know w'ot dat mean. Shark follow slave-ship all de way. Co-co see 'em, one day. Now he ready. Glad Loo-ard Island men come. Co-co help."

"Slave-ship?" thought Guert. "There hasn't been one of 'em here in a long while. New York folks don't want any more wild black men. Not since the bloody rising. So mother says. Three of hers were hung then. Awful! But there won't any be landed here. What do he and old Up-na-tan mean?"

They seemed to mean bluefishing, but it would

soon be too dark for that; and still the *Petrel* was tacking back and forth, with very fair sport for her crew, but farther and farther from Manhattan Island, and from the home supper-table, which Guert was longing for with an increasingly sharp appetite.

"Up-na-tan," he said suddenly, "look! There's a two-master lying this side o' the Kill von Kull, toward the reef. What on earth could make 'em anchor there?"

"Ugh!" grunted the Indian. "Heap shark."

Guert just then heard a sound of gritting teeth, and turned his head; but he turned away again, for he did not feel like saying anything to a face like that with which Co-co was glaring at the anchored schooner toward which the *Petrel* was tacking.

It was a tack to windward, and the boat was now pitching so that the fishing-lines were pulled in. They had really taken a fine catch of bluefish, if the takers could succeed in getting them to market without being punished for boat-stealing.

"What a strange smell," remarked Guert, as they swept nearer, and the wind came to them across the schooner. "I can see the sharks now. They are tearing something. Floundering."

"Keep away!" came down the wind, in a hoarse, threatening voice.

Almost instantly the *Petrel* changed her course, and sped away in another direction; but the Ashantee

"WE MUST ALL SPIN, MAUD. I DON'T WANT TO WEAR A YARD OF ANYTHING MADE IN ENGLAND."

spoke fiercely, in rough gutturals, to Up-na-tan, and the Indian responded as fiercely. All that Guert could understand was:

"Co-co know all he want."

"Shark eat heap dis time. Glad see plenty shark. So, so! Up-na-tan!"

His temper seemed cooler than that of his black friend; but it was all as yet a deep mystery to Guert Ten Eyck. He might have understood some things better, perhaps, if he could have known what was taking place miles and miles behind him.

Maud Wolcott met no wayfarers as she hurried along, up and across the dusty Bloomingdale Road. Probably everybody who could be down in the city was away from home that day. She came to a roadside gate that stood invitingly open. So did the door in the middle of a long, low stoop at the head of the walk, and she tripped on into the house without knocking; but she exclaimed inquiringly:

"Mrs. Ten Eyck?"

"This way, dear. Come right in," responded a voice from a room behind the little parlor at the left of the entry.

"Mrs. Ten Eyck, has Guert gotten home? What did they do with the tea?"

"Guert has not returned," replied Mrs. Ten Eyck, in a very thoughtful tone. "I fear there is trouble in the city. It is getting late."

"Oh! I wish he would come," said Maud excitedly; but if Mrs. Ten Eyck were under any uncommon excitement, her only expression of it was the exceeding rapidity and industry with which she plied her tall spinning-wheel, stepping back and forth with a lightness of foot and quickness of hand which may have meant something more than mere skill.

In a roomy alcove at the right, behind the entry and its twisting stairway, stood a large loom, and Mrs. Ten Eyck glanced at it as she remarked:

"We must all spin, Maud. American women must all be weavers. We must make our own cloth. I don't want to wear a yard of anything that is made in England."

"So mother says," said Maud. "We can all spin, and we can weave, too — mother, and both of my aunts and my grandmother. I can weave. The trouble is about the carding, and we haven't sheep enough."

"I wish there were not so many dogs," said Mrs. Ten Eyck. "They keep down the flocks. The wolves, too, are awful up the river and in the Mohawk valley. I suppose it's just so in New England. What between Indians and wild beasts and redcoats and King George" —

She was interrupted by a loud knocking at the outer door, and she stopped her wheel to follow Maud's hasty-going feet. She was only half-way through the parlor when she heard her young friend almost shout:

"Aleck Hamilton, what did the Liberty Boys do with the tea?"

"Threw it into the harbor," replied a boyish voice, as full of eagerness as her own. "Aaron Burr and I stood on the pier" —

"Hurrah!" began Maud, but Mrs. Ten Eyck stepped past her, and held out a hand to a second young gentleman, who had been detained a moment to hitch his pony at the gate, but who now walked in.

"I am glad to see you, Mr. Burr," she said. "How are your father and mother?"

Hospitality required so much of a formal welcome; but the two boys were compelled to make an effort in preserving their own good manners. Perhaps they were helped by the great dignity with which Mrs. Ten Eyck seemed to assert her social position, in spite of the evident plainness of her circumstances. Her house was small and farm-like, and there was only a moderately good farm behind it, but there was nothing humble in the ways of the patriotic mistress of the domain.

Aaron Burr replied gracefully as to his family, and added:

"I came over to get some books for father, just arrived from London. I've sent them on by a carrier, and came up this way on another errand, to one of his friends."

"But you saw them throw the tea overboard?"

burst from the lips of Mrs. Ten Eyck. "Was there any fighting?"

"Was Guert there?" asked Maud.

"No; no fighting," said Aaron.

"I saw Guert in one of the boats," said Hamilton. "Aaron didn't know. There's to be a great meeting called."

"How will they like this in Newark?" asked Mrs. Ten Eyck.

Aleck Hamilton was the shorter and slighter of the two boys. He seemed only a year or so older than Guert, but Aaron looked fully eighteen and mature for his age. He had, too, a peculiar polish and suavity of manner, considering how full his young face was of courage, if not of headlong self-will.

"The Jersey men will be ready," he said; "but I'm coming over again in a few weeks. Father says — we all say — there must be news from Boston by that time. We don't get it quickly enough. Don't know what's going on."

"There'll be news from Connecticut, too," said Maud. "We won't take any of their tea. They can't land any at New London. Young Mr. De Lancey says we are all rebels. We ought to be put down by the redcoats."

There was a fierce flash in the eyes of Aaron Burr as he responded:

"Miss Wolcott, if it comes to that, I'm a Connecticut man. I'm coming to fight under Old Put!"

"Thee mustn't talk treason," exclaimed a strong and sharply sarcastic voice behind them. "Thee must submit thyself to thy king and to his servants, and thee must swallow his tea; but if thee wants to go and visit with that good man Israel Putnam, Rachel Tarns will pay thy expenses."

"Rachel," laughed Mrs. Ten Eyck, "you are not a good Quaker. What have you to do with young rebels?"

"That is none of thy business, Anneke Ten Eyck," replied the Quakeress grimly. "What I came here for was to find out about the landing of that tea. Were all our men such cowards that they did not dare" —

There was fun in Aleck Hamilton as well as in Maud, for they burst into peals of laughter, joined by Aaron, shouting: "The tea is all in the East River!"

"God be praised!" said Rachel earnestly. "We must submit to the powers that be, but I'd shed the last drop of my blood" —

There she paused, and there was a swift exchange of questions and answers, while the boys filled up the first bare outlines of their news with ample and graphic accounts of the manner in which the East River had been turned into a teapot.

Long before that conversation began, there had been something else which might have interested Guert Ten Eyck if he had known it.

Very quickly after the departure of Co-co and

Up-na-tan, the huge, smoky, low-ceilinged kitchen of Mom Van Boom's Shark's Head Tavern was worth looking into. All the remarkable sailors with whom the negro and the Indian had been in council were there. Mom Van Boom and a colored helper were busily supplying them with fried perch and bullheads, and these were disappearing as fast as they came from the pan. The specially noteworthy point was the perfect order maintained by these men. They were all but silent, and what little they said was in the low, quick tones of men upon urgent business. They finished their fish, paid their score, and then, in squads of not more than three together, they left the tavern and strolled away, up the winding shore line. There was nothing singular in that, and perhaps there was not in the fact that when the great, scow-built ferry-boat, at the foot of Wall Street, hoisted her clumsy sail and put out toward the Brooklyn side, all of those strange fellows were on board of her.

They were as quiet as so many sheep, and when the boat reached the landing they went ashore, and pushed right on through the little village of Brooklyn and out into the open country, taking the road toward the southerly end of Long Island. If any craft which they belonged to were lying away down there in the Lower Bay, it must have been because she had some reason for not sailing in through the Narrows and up to the wharves of New York.

Guert was not just now thinking of things behind him. He was rather becoming unpleasantly curious about what might be before him.

"There must be something awful going on," he said to himself. "I've heard all about the slave-trade. The traders steal them in Africa. Of course Co-co hates them. They stole him. He'd like to kill them all. Up-na-tan would like to kill anything. But what ever made a slaver run into New York Harbor? She must have been running away from somebody."

That might be; but he knew it was of no use to ask questions, and so he only sat and thought as the *Petrel* went swiftly on. He watched as well as waited, and he took notice that each of his savage friends was now armed as they had not been on shore. Each had taken from somewhere under his clothing, and had fastened in his belt, very long and dangerous-looking sheath-knives and a brace of pistols.

Up-na-tan had seemed to take his out from among the ample fringes of his leggings, while Co co had reached over his shoulder and had pulled out his weapons from below the nape of his neck. Guert saw the Indian touch the handle of his weapon once, and thought he heard him say, as he withdrew his hand:

"No; boy all right. No tell. Take him home safe. Up-na-tan keep promise."

Co-co had also touched his knife hilt at the same moment, but his muttered remark came a breath later:

"Chief right," he said. "Co-co take care of he young frien';" but he turned to Guert and added:

"No use for tell. Yo, yo! Wait an' see. Nebber want to tell, Co-co t'ink. Git he t'roat cut, suah."

Guert felt called upon to reply:

"Tell you what, I sha'n't tell; but I do hate any kind of slaver. They ought to be all hung."

"Dat's de talk!" exclaimed Co-co. "Heah dat, Up-na-tan? He keep he mouf shut. No use tell, anyhow."

So far, the most important secret troubling Guert's mind was the fact that he had stolen Steven De Lancey's yacht. He was not likely to tell about that, he thought.

Now at last the *Petrel* was dancing along over the rougher water of the Lower Bay; but she was keeping well in toward the Long Island shore. It was getting very dusky, but Guert believed that he could dimly see something like a pair of masts against the dark background of a patch of tall trees.

"They say it's good anchorage," he thought; "but hardly anything ever stops here. Wonder what it is."

The next thing he seemed to see was a boat full of men putting out from the shore; but he was called away from staring at her by a hoarse hail that startled him, it was so near.

"We're almost aboard that schooner," he exclaimed; but the hail was promptly replied to by Up-na-tan.

"Halloo!" said Guert. "I've heard him do that before. He said it was the war-whoop of the Iroquois. It's an awful screech. Hark! There's a fellow in that boat that can do it. Hear Co-co!"

The Indian war-whoop was not any more horribly shrill and ferocious than was the yell of the Ashantee; but another shout from the schooner and another from the boat seemed to be full of fierce exultation. Then Guert knew that Up-na-tan said, in Dutch:

"We found her. She is lying this side of the Kill von Kull. You can run right in and get her. She does not carry any deck gun, and her foremast is broken at the cap. She can't get away."

"We are alongside now," groaned Guert. "I won't go on board, but I'll look."

Up-na-tan and Co-co told him to stay in the *Petrel*, but they went over the starboard side into the schooner just as the boat from shore landed its passengers directly opposite; and twice as many more men, of similar patterns, were waiting to meet them.

Rough as they looked, they were not at all noisy; and nobody paid Guert any attention as he anxiously, excitedly, peered over from the half-deck of the *Petrel*.

"I'm not afraid," he said to himself; "but I do feel queer. She's a pirate."

The crew looked like it, but that was by no means all. Low as the schooner looked from the water, her bulwarks were very high and strong, and they were pierced with ports for the four guns ranged on each side.

"I guess they are long six-pounders," said Guert to himself; "and that swivel-gun amidships is a long eighteen. See the pikes and cutlasses and muskets at the masts! Awful! I've seen a pirate."

He had only a moment to look, for her crew were lifting her anchor, and in a minute or so Up-na-tan and Co-co were back in the *Petrel.*

"Off, quick!" said Up-na-tan. "Ole Portingee say t'row boy overboard!"

There was indeed a fierce, half-hushed discussion among a group near the swivel-gun, and there was a sudden movement just as the *Petrel* swung her head clear and darted away. Hoarse hails followed her; but Up-na-tan's reply may have been the whoop of the Manhattans for all Guert knew. That of Co-co was only a derisive "Yo, yo! Nebber ketch dis boat."

"Can't they?" asked Guert; but there was no reply except the very practical fact that the *Petrel* was running swiftly homeward while the pirates were getting up their anchor. They may have had good reasons for not wishing to use any noisy gunpowder just then.

"Pirates?" said Guert to himself. "They say the West India Islands swarm with them. Getting as bad as they were in Kidd's time. The British men-o'-war ought to hunt them down. I s'pose they will, some day."

On went the *Petrel* in the deepening gloom, through the Narrows, into the upper New York Bay; and now Guert felt better, but he kept a sharp lookout behind them.

"There she is!" he exclaimed at length. "There comes the pirate."

In a moment more he added to himself:

"She's not chasing us. She is passing us. We are both running toward the slaver."

Then he held his breath, for down the wind came loud, angry shouts and yells, followed by two cannon reports and a rattle of musketry shots.

"There!" he almost gasped. "They have boarded her. It's a fight."

"Dey on'y shoot a leetle. Yo, yo!" hoarsely chuckled the Ashantee. "Dey won't leab one ob 'em. Kill 'em all. Dey kill, too."

"Bof kill heap," snarled Up-na-tan fiercely. "Too many ole Kidd men. Shark get 'em all some day. Shark eat shark. T'row 'em overboard."

"Co-co wish he had dem Congo men to work he big farm," remarked Co-co. "Now ole pirate sell 'em all in Cuba. Slabe-ship bes' kine ob prize for Kidd men."

Guert understood that neither of his friends had acted from any love of freedom for its own sake. They had only been willing to act as pilot-fish, to help one kind of sharks to destroy another. He was very glad indeed, however, that the *Petrel* was so swift, and that she was homeward bound. His delight was great when she reached the Albany pier and was tied up. He almost ran toward Whitehall Street, while Co-co and Up-na-tan slipped away in the dark with their bluefish.

"I've seen a slaver and a pirate," he said to himself; and he seemed to have forgotten about the tea-ship.

CHAPTER III.

THE PRESS-GANG AND THE NOANK.

MAUD WOLCOTT did not have a very long visit that day at the Ten Eyck homestead. Not only did Aaron Burr and Aleck Hamilton hurry away, but Maud felt that it was her duty to carry all the news at once to Mrs. Murray.

That patriotic lady was indeed waiting for it in a fever of expectation; and so were other people, for whose comfort Rachel Tarns herself shortly marched away, remarking:

"Anneke, if Guert brings thee anything of importance, thee can send him to my house. Thee may tell him I am glad he went in his boat with those good men. Our people will not now be tempted with that tea."

Mrs. Ten Eyck found herself alone, but in a greater anxiety and a harder waiting time than any of them; for hour after hour went by and her son did not return. All sorts of imaginations troubled her as to what might have become of him. There had been no fighting, no violence; only a great tea-making; but why did not Guert come home?

"Can they have captured him? He is only a boy," she all but groaned. "O, dear! Now I know how mothers feel when their sons have been impressed for the navy. What if they have kept him?"

Against that idea was the fact that no British ships-of-war were in the harbor, although there were several cruisers off the coast, and a squadron was expected to arrive shortly.

Her heart grew heavier and heavier as the long hours went by; but she was not the only person whose burden was unusual.

Even Co-co and Up-na-tan had all the bluefish they could carry when they left the *Petrel* at the wharf and stalked off to deliver their cargo at Mom Van Boom's. They were very strong men, and they did not seem to know anything about weariness; but it was not so with poor Guert.

He had never before, in all his life, felt so completely weighed down. He had had no dinner, no supper; he had pulled in heavy fish; he had sailed fast and far; but all that was as nothing to the weight of the secret he was carrying. He felt sure his life depended upon keeping it; but that did not tend to raise his spirits as he plodded along the Bowery Lane homeward.

The people of New York were nearly all asleep, after

the intense excitement of their first open rebellion against their lawful king and his ministers. Some of them may have been lying awake, wondering what would be the end of it all; but not many were sitting at windows and watching, as was Mrs. Ten Eyck; she did not try to know how late.

At last she sprang to her feet, exclaiming:

"Thank God! there he is."

She had seen somebody pause for a moment at the gate; but she did not know how Guert all but staggered as he lifted the latch, and she did not hear him say:

"The only way for me to keep it is to get mother to help. She's just the right kind of woman."

There was no doubt of that, and in a moment more she was hugging him, in the entry, and was asking him where he had been and if he had had anything to eat.

"Oh! but ain't I glad to get home," was the substance of what he had to say, to begin with, but after that the entire story of the cruise of the *Petrel* came out, from beginning to end Mrs. Ten Eyck listened, with many motherly comments and counsels.

"Slavers? Pirates?" she exclaimed, at last. "Why, Guert, all you've got to say is not to say anything. I hope they all killed each other."

"Up-na-tan and Co-co seem to think that's what they did," said Guert, but he was not nearly so hungry now, for he had been eating as well as talking.

"Now, go to bed," said his mother. "You needn't get up till you want to. Oh! how glad I am you are back safe."

He was too tired to be very glad, but for all that he was up and dressed only a little later than usual, next morning. Perhaps it was as well, for he had hardly eaten his breakfast before he heard the voice of Maud Wolcott in the parlor asking:

"Has Guert come home?"

He also heard another voice remarking:

"Anneke, thee lets thy son have too much liberty. Thee is not strict enough in thy government. Thee should make him come home at sunset."

"I'm no chicken, Rachel," said Guert, as he walked into the room.

"Thee is a bad boy," said Rachel. "Thee put thy good king's tea into the salt water. Thee does not know how to make tea. Tell us how thee did it — thee and thy wicked associates."

Guert had to tell, and he was entirely willing, if only to keep off too many questions as to what made him stay away so late.

"Thee broke open the first chest, thee bad boy!" exclaimed Rachel admiringly. "What if thy good king had been in that box?"

"Rachel," said Mrs. Ten Eyck, "it's well he wasn't, if you had been there. You would have thrown him overboard."

"Guert needn't be so proud of it," said Maud. "The Boston men set the example. What are eighteen chests of tea? Our Mohawks emptied hundreds of them into the harbor."

"You're not a Boston girl," said Guert. "You're only from Connecticut. You haven't done anything."

"It's all the same," said Maud, with some spirit. "They don't dare to bring us any. We'll show you!"

"Tell you what," said Guert, "it was too bad. Every man was sick about it because there were so few of 'em. They hunted and hunted for more chests, but there weren't any."

That was the spirit of the whole town, that day, and through all the days that followed.

One of the most curious features of the situation, even to Guert, was the fact that nobody seemed to be aware that anything like a slaver or a pirate had been seen in the harbor. There were, indeed, dark rumors of merchant ships that were missing, but that was no rare matter, in those days. Perhaps another noteworthy oddity was the strange willingness of one Indian and one black man to work pretty steadily in Mrs. Ten Eyck's cornfield. Not that laborers were scarce, but then Co-co and Up-na-tan had not been known as steady workers.

The whole community was in a continual ferment. There were public as well as secret meetings of the

Liberty Boys, the Mohawks, and the Committee of Fifty-one. There were riotous collisions between the citizens and the British garrison of Fort George, but the cooler heads on both sides prevented anything very serious. Guert had been more than a little grieved at missing some of the best of these affairs while out fishing with Co-co, but he had a compensation, for he had rowed all around each of three British men-of-war that were now anchored in the harbor. He did not tell anybody but his mother that the Ashantee remarked:

"Yo, yo! Up-na-tan say tie 'em up to canoe-load o' powder an' blow 'em sky high, some day. Dat ole Indian got a heap o' bad in him. Say de king stole he island."

The worst of it all was the lack of news and the ragged quality of any that came. There were so many mere rumors that nobody knew what to believe. Guert knew that the king and parliament of England had shut up the port of Boston, but he could not quite understand it, even when Aleck Hamilton tried to explain it to him; and he felt as indignant as did Maud Wolcott herself, when he carried that news to the Murray mansion.

"Do come often," said Mrs. Murray. "Come every time you hear anything. Why, Guert, you seem to learn more than anybody else does."

Perhaps that was because he felt a great and growing thirst to know what was going on. In fact, he seemed to feed on it and it made him grow taller. It also made him go down town more and more often, especially as Mrs. Ten Eyck herself, with the help of Rachel Tarns, had almost daily errands to send him on.

"Thee is a good boy," said Rachel. "Thee is willing to go all the way to the Battery to buy me a four pennorth o' pins in Pearl Street."

So it came to pass, one morning, that the Murray family carriage pulled up on the eastern side of Whitehall Street, just as Maud exclaimed :

"Aunt Wolcott, there he is. There is Guert, talking to that other boy, over there on the Bowling Green by King George's statue."

"I wish I could call him," said Mrs. Murray. "There is something new stirring. I know there is."

"What is it, Mrs. Murray?" asked a tall and stately gentleman, who had paused and lifted his cocked hat at the side of the carriage. "Can I be of any service?"

"Thank you, Mr. Livingston; we were only thinking of the news," replied Mrs. Murray. "Is there any?"

"None of importance," he said, and he went on to report whatever he knew; but Maud was watching Guert, although she could not hear him, for he was evidently much interested about something.

"Think of the heft of him," Guert was saying to

the other boy, as they both looked up at the statue. "What do you s'pose he'd weigh, now?—all that brass."

"What wud he weigh, indade? And he's not bross at all. He's nothin' but lead, hoss and mon, painted wid bross."

"Lead's heavier'n brass, Pat Mahon," said Guert. "How did they ever set him up?"

"Set him oop? I saw thim," responded Pat. "He's holler. If he hadn't been holler they'd niver ha' h'isted him. There's nothin' in him but wind."

There he sat, on his leaden steed, the great equestrian statue of King George III., in the middle of the Bowling Green.

"I knew it was hollow," said Guert, but no uninformed observer would have known but what he was made of bronze, or at least of cannon metal, although there was a great deal that was heavy about him, even in the expression of his face.

Guert Ten Eyck and his friend seemed to have some special reason for inspecting that statue, for Pat Mahon shortly remarked:

"He's the king, indade, but he's no call to be king in owld Oireland. Me mother towld me they shtole it."

"He's the King in England," responded Guert; "but what's he got to do with the Ten Eycks, or anybody here? This isn't England, it's America."

"THINK OF THE HEFT OF HIM," SAID GUERT.

"Nathan!" exclaimed a shrill woman's voice near them. "Hear them! Even the boys are full of treason. Neither of them is over fifteen. Think of them talking against the king!"

"One of them is Dutch, Aunt Sapphira," replied Nathan, "and the other is Irish, and I'm a Yankee. What have either of us to do with English kings, three thousand miles away! Guert Ten Eyck is right. This is America! What's that? Look! Infamous! It's a press-gang. If they haven't seized one of my own neighbors! Lyme Avery, they've no right to take you. You are skipper of your own craft."

On the westerly side of the Bowling Green ran Broadway, down to the grassy level of the Battery parade ground. On the east ran Whitehall Street, and both were lined with aristocratic residences. Guert and Pat had turned, almost open-mouthed, to stare at the double file of British man-o'-war's-men which had halted on the Broadway sidewalk near the Green. There were nearly a dozen of them, headed by a sprightly midshipman and a burly, scowling boatswain, their real commander. Handcuffed and elbow-fettered, two and two, between the guarding files of armed sailors, were eight unlucky victims of the press-gang system, and it was one of these who had been spoken to by the tall, intellectual youth at whose side Aunt Sapphira was standing. The captives were all, apparently, seafaring men, but this one did not seem, in dress or bearing, like a common sailor. His face was furiously red as he responded:

"So I told them, Nathan Hale. The *Noank's* at her wharf in the East River, and I'm her owner. Little they care for our rights."

"Shut up!" roared the boatswain, dealing him a heavy blow on the mouth. "And if that lubber doesn't hold his jaw, I'll take him along."

"No, you won't," sternly replied the young man. "I shall at once protest against your taking Skipper Avery. It's contrary to law."

"He'll go aboard the *Tigress* and so will you," piped the midshipman, in youthful imitation of the boatswain's authority and brutality.

"It's of no use," said Hale to himself, in a low voice. "We can do nothing. We are bound, hand and foot."

"Ugh!" exclaimed a deep, wrathful growl behind him. "Press wrong man? Press Up-na-tan, one time. Flog him one year."

Guert's eyes were glancing from one face to the other of those two men, in spite of his fierce indignation concerning the seizure of American sailors. He knew how the Manhattan's face could look at times, but it seemed as if, just now, it expressed all the tigerish ferocity of all the red men. In strong contrast, as if belonging to another world, was the splendid young manhood of Nathan Hale. Six feet high, broad-shouldered, muscular, erect, with bright blue eyes, rosy complexion, light brown curling hair, easy and graceful carriage, his voice had rung out like a trumpet in defying the boatswain. He turned, only an instant, to the Manhattan, saying:

"You escaped? You got away?"

"No," replied Up-na-tan, with a lurid gleam on his tattooed wrinkles. "No-got away. Ship got away. Ship go to bottom one day. Indian here. So, so! Up-na-tan! Tell him send ship to bottom."

"Nathan," shouted Avery, at that moment, "go to the *Noank* and tell my wife and sons that these wolves have gotten me. Tell them to sail for home. They will hear from me in some way. Tell the boys to get good guns and be ready to join Old Put. Our time's coming."

"I'll tell them," replied Hale. "My gun's ready now. So am I."

"Treason!" almost screamed Aunt Sapphira.

"Treason!" echoed the middy. "Bo's'n, arrest that man."

"The lubber's geared beyond our reach," growled the boatswain. "We don't want him. March, men!"

"O, Lord!" groaned Skipper Avery, as he was forced to move on; and he again shouted:

"Good-by, Nathan! See my wife. Tell her. Tell the boys I'll come or I'll die trying. There'll be blood for this."

Guert was again staring at the heroically handsome face of Nathan Hale. It seemed all lit up as he responded :

"Good-by, Lyme ! There'll be blood for all these things."

"Silence, Hale," said another speaker. "Our time is not yet come."

"Judge Livingston" — was all Hale could say ; but over at the carriage he had left, Maud was leaning angrily out, for she understood it now, and so did Mrs. Murray.

"They won't take Guert," she said, "will they? They won't take anybody else? It's horrible! But isn't that man splendid!"

"Hark!" said Mrs. Murray. "Oh! it is too bad. He sent word to his family" —

"Captain," just then eagerly exclaimed Guert, and he spoke to Hale, "look! The lobsters are coming."

"That's our trouble just now," said Livingston. "No use to protest. Your friend will be on board the *Tigress,* and she will be at sea, before we could do anything."

The boatswain was saying to the Yankee skipper, with a heavy blow :

"You'll desert, will you? A cat-o'-nine-tails'll take the mutiny out o' ye!"

Hale and Livingston looked, as Guert pointed down the street. There were not many of Guert's "lobsters." Only a couple of companies of British soldiers on parade, and they were now marching out and up Broadway, preceded by a fife and drum. They were fine, soldierly-looking fellows, in perfect equipment and capital drill; the very men to win a battle with.

"Hale," said Livingston, "when our militia can step off like that, we can hope to do something."

"I don't know," slowly responded Hale. "Braddock went into the woods with an army of just such troops. All that came out with any credit were the Virginia militia and Colonel Washington. I must go to the *Noank*. I'll sail home on her. The Avery boys'll fight some day for this. So will I."

"Don't ye do it, Nathan," exclaimed Aunt Sapphira. "Don't ye ever turn traitor to your king."

"I'm for my country first," he said sternly. "I'm ashamed of any American woman that is not."

"So am I!" came in an excited voice from a carriage which had been driven quickly around the head of the Green and halted near them. "I'm for my country, sir."

"O, Aunt Murray!" exclaimed Maud; "I'm so glad you said it. I didn't dare to."

"I'm against treason," angrily replied Aunt Sapphira. "No traitor is of any kin to me. You'll be hung for treason yet, Nathan Hale. So will all your rebel crew. Serve you right, too; and I'll furnish the rope."

She was a woman with a peculiarly set and bitter expression of face; but her present lack of self-control was a good expression of the heated state of feeling on both sides of the controversy. People were beginning to hate one another.

"Good-by, then," said her handsome young relative. "I'm no traitor, nor rebel; but we Americans must stand up for our rights."

"Or we shall have none at all, soon," sadly remarked Livingston; but just then Maud was loudly whispering from the carriage:

"That's right, Aleck. Speak to him."

Hale was turning away when he was confronted by a slender, but very intelligent youth, who held out a hand, hurriedly addressing him with: "I'm Aleck Hamilton. Glad to meet you. Heard of you before. No use. We can do nothing for your friend."

"Nothing," said Hale, grasping the proffered hand. "We shall meet again. I must make haste now."

"The New York boys are ready," said Hamilton. "We'll show you."

"The great trouble is a leaden king," said Hale, pointing at the statue; and then he strode away, followed closely by Guert, but Pat Mahon had marched up Broadway with the soldiers.

"Tyranny! oppression!" said Mrs. Murray to Livingston. "How long are our people to endure these things?"

"I don't know," replied the gloomy-faced patriot. "I can't talk now, madam. 'On the part of their oppressors there was power,' it is written."

"Bad power breaks," said Mrs. Murray.

Guert felt a hand on his arm and turned, while Up-na-tan pointed at Hale.

"Ugh!" he grunted. "Look! Young chief! Heap man! Take 'calp some day. Up-na-tan like him. Heap fight."

He did not follow further, and Guert felt even more awed than before; but he had an idea flashing through his head, and he caught up with Hale.

"Sir, sir!" he said eagerly, "I'll go to the *Noank* with you. I know where she is. But there's barrels o' powder at the wharf-end, beyond the *Noank*. Just out o' the battery store, for one o' the ships."

"No use, my brave boy," said Hale.

"Yes, you could," said Guert. "'Tisn't half guarded."

"We shall need powder," muttered Hale, as he strode thoughtfully onward. "How many barrels of King George's powder would pay us for Lyme Avery?"

"I'll go and see what they do with him," said Guert, "and then I'll come to the *Noank*."

Just then Mrs. Murray was saying to Maud, as the carriage rolled along:

"Anyhow, we shall know all about it when Guert comes home."

"I'll go over to Mrs. Ten Eyck's and find out," said Maud. "Guert will know."

Easterly from Whitehall slip, at no great distance, a long wooden pier ran out into deep water, and beyond it was a broad basin and another pier. At this second pier lay a saucy, trim-looking schooner, of about four hundred tons, with the word *Noank* painted on her stern.

Away out in the middle of the East River lay the *Tigress* frigate, waiting for stores from the government warehouses, and for such re-enforcements of seamen as her merciless press-gangs might steal for her among the merchant-shipping and along the shore.

Down to the water's edge at the Battery hurried the party of man-hunters which had charge of Skipper Avery.

"Take off their irons," commanded a navy lieutenant, who inspected the captives and who replied with a sneer and a threat to the protest of the owner of the *Noank*. "I can spare you but two men. The pressed men must row. Shoot the first mutineer. It is no time for nonsense."

He spoke to the coxswain in charge of a mere cockle-shell of a yawl-boat, not more than large enough for six men, and now to carry eleven, but he thereby put an oar into the strong hands of Lyme Avery.

"I'll swamp her," growled the angry skipper to himself. "See 'f I don't. I hope they can all swim. I can."

Guert was near enough on the shore to see what was done, but he could not hear the skipper think.

"Guess Mr. Hale has boarded the *Noank*," he said aloud, as he glanced up the shore. "She's going. I'll watch that boat."

The *Noank* had indeed cast loose and something was doing with her mainsail, but she was not yet headed up the river toward New London. She had been all ready for a start and was only waiting the arrival of her commander, when Nathan Hale stepped on board with the disastrous news of his captivity. It was an utterly unexpected cup of gall and wormwood for the wife and the two nearly grown-up sons of the impressed man, but, right in the midst of their expressions of grief and indignation, Hale glanced across the basin at the other wharf and exclaimed:

"The powder!"

He hardly added ten words of explanation before Mrs. Avery sobbed out:

"O, boys! Yes! Get the king's powder. We mustn't miss that. I hope you'll have a chance to use it all."

In a moment more, the *Noank* was sweeping toward the other pier where, by some recklessness or other, four barrels were waiting, unguarded, like so many passengers.

Guert watched the overloaded yawl. There was only a moderate sea running and she seemed safe enough, even if some water did dash in. The *Noank* had barely reached the lower pier, however, when a great cry rang out across the water, from away beyond Whitehall slip.

"Quick, boys," said Mrs. Avery, weeping bitterly. "Roll that nearest barr'l right on board."

Just as an overgrown wave lifted the press-gang yawl, a stalwart oarsman on its port side had put all his strength into his oar, sinking it deep, "caught a crab," grasped the next man, lurched heavily over, and in a moment the boat had capsized.

It was a lubberly performance, but still it was very well done.

There was no mutiny nor could there be any shooting by a coxswain whose musket was under water.

Strong were the arms of Skipper Avery, and strong, too, was the rushing tide which bore him away while his late boatmates struggled around their swamped yawl and shouted for help, and while Guert Ten Eyck ran his best toward the *Noank*.

"Rope!" he shouted, as he sprang on board. "He's coming this way. Rope!"

"I understand," said Nathan Hale. "I see him."

The tide from New York Bay was not a servant of King George. Neither was the long whaling line thrown out, a minute later, by the old harpooneer who served as mate of the *Noank*.

Two other Yankee seamen were lifting the mainsail

when the skipper was pulled on board, but Mrs. Avery and her sons and Guert were rolling along the last of the barrels of powder.

"Lyme!" she shouted, "it's gunpowder."

"Quick! In with it, wife," he sputtered. "We want it all. It's pretty near time to shoot."

Guert went on board with the barrel, the sail was up, the breeze freshened mightily, and away sprang the *Noank* like a race horse, up the East River, leaving behind her no man who knew precisely what she had for cargo.

CHAPTER IV.

THE CRUISE OF THE NOANK.

SKIPPER AVERY was a very wet man when his wife left the powder and threw her arms around him, and tried to express her gladness at his rescue and her hatred of the press-gang in one breath.

Guert looked back along their course and remarked:

"I guess none of those fellows got drowned. One boat went to them from the shore and another from the *Tigress.* I wonder if that brig is coming after us."

"They can't know that the skipper is on board," said the old harpooneer; "but I ain't so sartain about the powder, 'n that'd be a'most a hangin' matter."

"That's so," exclaimed Skipper Avery. "It's all marked with the king's broad-arrer brand; but we can put it overboard if they follow us. We'd better watch that brig. She's a ten-gun, though, and she can't catch the *Noank* in a fair race."

The rescue boat from the *Tigress* reached the capsized yawl first, and was itself quickly overcrowded.

"Are they all here? Count!" said the officer in command.

"One missing," replied the coxswain, in some dismay. "It's the New London skipper. He's an old whaler. He capsized us."

"Did he drown?"

"Niver a dhrown," said one of the other impressed men. "He wint off wid the toide, like he was a fish."

"He had to go ashore, then," said the officer. "We'll get him. We'll punish him for deserting, too. After we shoot a few of 'em, they'll know better than to try tricks on us."

The skipper had therefore been guilty of treason, or some other capital crime, in getting away and going home.

Not many minutes later, there was a tremendous disturbance on the Albany pier, for a stiff-looking sergeant was staring around him and stammering:

"It's all, all r-right, levtenant. The launch from the *Tigress* has been 'ere again. They've took away the last borril o' th' powd'r."

"I'll report them!" stormed the lieutenant. "It's all out of order. They'd no right to take a pound of it without giving a receipt. No naval officer seems to know what his duty is."

Nevertheless, one naval officer, with a telescope in his hand, on board the ten-gun brig, had seen Skipper Avery's escape and the seizure of the barrels, and had deemed it his duty to overhaul that schooner. His own craft had already been ordered on cruising duty, and was ready for sea, so that no time was lost — not even in his rapid exchange of signals with the captain of the *Tigress.*

"Catch her," he was signalled back. "Sink her or burn her. Impress the whole crew."

"Wife," said Skipper Avery, as the *Noank* shot into the channel between Blackwell's Island and the Long Island shore, "this is colony powder now. If Old Put'll give us some guns one of these days, six-pounders and a long gun, we'll turn the *Noank* into a cruiser. She can outsail anything they've got."

"It will come to that," said Nathan Hale; "but they would call colonial cruisers pirates."

"It'll go down into the hold now, any way," replied the skipper, and he turned to Guert as he added: "My boy, we can't put you ashore now. You've got to make the trip to New London."

Guert thought of his mother, and he almost felt queer in his throat, in spite of his excitement in watching the British brig; but he responded:

"All right. I'll get home somehow."

"We'll send ye, safe and sound," said the skipper cheerily.

Nevertheless, at that very moment Mrs. Ten Eyck was looking with intense anxiety into the beaming black face of Co-co, while he reported:

"Guert's all right, Missus. I seen him. De skipper, he upsot de yawl. Swum to de schoonah. Guert, he help. Dey hook de powder bar'ls. Den dey sail away, an' Guert, he go to New Lon'on."

"Boy heap young chief," said Up-na-tan, standing behind Co-co.

"God will take care of him," said his mother mournfully. "It was a dreadfully daring thing to take the powder."

There was no doubt of that, and the theft from the king's army and navy would have to be prudently concealed, lest the *Noank* should be confiscated and her crew hanged or impressed; but, not much later, when Maud came over to learn the news, she found Rachel Tarns there in a state of strange exultation.

"Thee need not fear Maud, Anneke," almost burst from the stern lips of the triumphant Quakeress. "Maud is a good girl. She will be glad that wicked and violent men have four barrels less of gunpowder to shoot with."

"Maud," exclaimed Mrs. Ten Eyck, "Guert has gone away off to New London."

It all came out then, and Maud herself had a great deal to tell about the press-gang and its captives, and Nathan Hale.

"Didn't he look handsome!" she said. "He was splendid. So was Guert. He'll have a grand time."

"I do hope and trust they won't get him," groaned

Mrs. Ten Eyck. "It's the wickedest thing. Stealing men! It's worse than taxing tea."

"Anneke," said Rachel Tarns, "thee should not speak lightly of thy good king. He needs seafaring men for the ships that must protect thee from the French and from the red men; and if he wants thy boy, thee must not murmur. It is treason."

"Girls can't be impressed for sailors," said Maud to herself, as she hurried away to tell Mrs. Murray the news; "but I wish King George could be. Anyhow, I'm glad they got the powder."

Nevertheless, those four barrels were the worst part of the danger now besetting Skipper Avery and the *Noank*. Having on board a deserter, or even being one, was not half so bad as out and out treason coopered up in that shape.

The ten-gun brig was not at all a slow boat, and proved it as soon as her sails were spread; but the *Noank* had the start of her.

"If I had a boat," said Guert, "you could put me ashore."

"Haven't one to spare," said the skipper, "and it won't do for us to lose a tack, or we'd run in and land ye. That feller'll race us for all we're wuth."

They were going through the tossing waters of the Hell Gate channel now, and it was well for the *Noank* that the old harpooneer at her helm knew every rock of that perilous passage. Guert almost forgot his mother's anxiety about him, as he leaned over the prow and watched the foaming eddies among which the schooner was dashing onward.

"That brig'll need a good pilot," remarked Nathan Hale. "We shall gain on her, here."

That was the very thing that shortly vexed the soul of the British commander. His pilot was doubtless a good one, but he was a Rhode Island Yankee and he insisted upon being exceedingly careful of the craft he was steering. He picked his way along, and in and out, tacking and rock-dodging, with the utmost fidelity, while the runaway *Noank* spread her wide wings and sped away into the Sound beyond.

"We are away out of range or she'd send a shot after us," said the skipper to Hale. "If this breeze holds we shall reach New London before to-morrow night."

The young patriot was at that moment looking eastward, through a telescope he had brought up from the cabin.

"If that sail ahead is the *Merlin* man-o'-war," replied Hale, "I'm afraid we shall never get there. She is due at New York."

"I didn't know that," said the skipper calmly; "but I'm safe enough. You don't know the Long Island shore, and her captain'll only lose the *Merlin* if he follows the *Noank*. I'll show you."

Guert heard them, and a thrill went over him. He

was really at sea and he was beginning to feel as if he and all the rest of them were already at war with King George. On sped the light-heeled schooner, and further and dimmer grew the sails of the pursuing brig; but now they could see ahead of them, without any glass, growing larger and larger every moment, the spreading canvas of a large ship under full sail.

"The next tack'll bring us pretty nigh her, Lyme Avery," said the old harpooneer. "What'll ye do?"

"Run right for her," said the skipper, "and then scoot away across them Long Island shoals."

"That's the talk," said the grim sailor heartily. "If she follows us she'll git herself stuck. I'd like to lose one ship for King George this arternoon."

No doubt the officers of the *Merlin* were watching the swift approach of the Yankee schooner from the beginning, but now a heavily-made gentleman in uniform, on the quarter-deck, was remarking:

"Bring her to, lieutenant. Take out every man except just enough to sail her home. These whalers and coasters are just the men we want."

Lyme Avery knew that, and so did his wife, and sons, and his crew, and the two passengers, and some of them were almost holding their breaths as they measured the lessening distance between them and the gallant war-ship of their king.

If she had been a pirate they could not have felt more deeply that she was their most dangerous enemy.

Not a soul on board of her dreamed but what the *Noank* would obey the signal to come within hail which had been made to her, and she was evidently coming.

"What does she mean, though, by going to leeward of us?" suddenly exclaimed the captain of the *Merlin*. "Port your helm, there! Run out a gun! She has tacked away."

The great ship was slower in her movements than was the saucy schooner which had so unexpectedly dodged, but the gun was out quickly.

"Boom!" and the first shot struck the water not twenty yards from the stern of the *Noank*.

Boom! boom! boom! one after another roared out the angry thunder of the *Merlin*, but she had been only barely within range at first, and now it was but chance firing.

"If only a shot or so strikes us we may not suffer much," said Guert, but he knew very little about cannon; and Hale responded:

"It might smash a mast, or it might hit the powder and blow us up."

"That's so," said Guert, a little crestfallen. "Isn't she gaining on us?"

"Of course she is," remarked the skipper, behind them. "It'll be touch and go. There! somebody on board of her knows the coast. That was almost a broadside. How mad they are!"

It was so. The sailing-master of the *Merlin* was a

Cape Cod man, long since impressed from a whaler, and he had respectfully reported to the first lieutenant:

"Shoal water ahead, sir. That craft'll be aground before she knows it, and we can take her with boats."

"Shoaling?" almost screamed the lieutenant, but he instantly added a storm of orders, in response to which the good ship swung away from her supposed peril, while the sailing-master, who was thanked for saving her, went forward saying to himself:

"Them guns was almost a-reachin' of her. But it's jist as well we didn't run within a mile o' that there shoal."

"Dangerous navigation," said the captain of the *Merlin*. "We couldn't risk the ship, you know. We must have scored her. Hope she'll sink!"

The *Noank* was not scored, and she did not sink, but Nathan Hale remarked to Skipper Avery:

"It was very poor gunnery. The shot fell all around us, at first, and not one came on board."

"It wasn't because they didn't mean to hit," said the skipper. "They had the law on their side, too. For all they knew, we're pirates. They'd a parfect law jistification to blaze away."

"And murder us all," said his wife, "you and me and the boys, just for nothing?"

"It's sea law, Hanner," said the skipper; "but none of her shot kin tetch now."

As for Guert, he had a strong feeling, now it was

BOOM! BOOM! ROARED OUT THE ANGRY THUNDER OF THE MERLIN.

over, that he would not for anything have missed being cannonaded.

"I wish I could tell mother," he thought, "and then I just would like to tell Aleck Hamilton and Maud Wolcott. Wouldn't it make her mad? I guess it would Rachel Tarns, too."

He knew the strong-minded Quaker lady pretty well. She may not at that moment have been out of temper, but she was looking very vigorously into the faces of a knot of finely-dressed women in a shop on Beaver Street, away down town, and she was saying:

"Jane De Lancey, thee and thy king and thy governor are too much for me. I am so blind that I cannot see their wisdom. They drive men to take up carnal weapons" —

"I cannot hear such talk," began another woman, even more haughtily indignant than Miss De Lancey had seemed. "It ill becomes you, Rachel Tarns, considering how leniently you Quakers have been dealt with. You are permitted to practice your religious notions unmolested. Not one of you has been punished, and this is your gratitude!"

"Thy good king and his gentle governor have not hanged me, nor burned me, nor put me in prison, for serving God in my own way," said Rachel scornfully. "I will tell thee a thing, Antoinette Tryon. At the last meeting of Friends, there was a testimony concerning thy kinsman, the Governor of this province."

"What was it, if you dare to tell?" angrily demanded Miss Tryon.

"I do dare to tell thee," said Rachel, "and thee can make the most of it. One Friend was given to say and to testify that the man Tryon would be the last to call himself a king's governor on this Island of Manhattan."

"He ought to be hung for that, if he was not hung for being a Quaker," replied Miss Tryon; and Miss De Lancey added:

"Rachel Tarns! I'm ashamed of you."

"Thee need not be," said Rachel. "Thee should be glad to hear the news. But they could not hang him, if they dared."

"Why couldn't they?" demanded Miss Tryon.

"Because she is not a man, but a woman," said Rachel, "and she is nearly ninety years old. She also testified that the days of all the kings draw nigh unto an end. Thee can tell thy kinsman, Antoinette Tryon, that both Jane De Lancey and Rachel Tarns honor the king. I trust she will never commit treason. As for me, I am a woman of peace."

It was not precisely the expression of her face at that moment, but she picked up a bundle handed her by the shopman and walked away. Neither of the others would have done that, but it was against the precepts of the New York Quakers to own black men or women, and the richest of them were therefore often compelled to help themselves. Nothing easily imaginable would have induced Miss Tryon or Miss De Lancey to carry that bundle, but they were both bearing a great burden of angry loyalty, and they seemed to have sincere sympathy from others who had heard Rachel tell the dangerous prophecy. Things were indeed getting into a bad condition when tea could be thrown overboard, soldiers pelted in Broadway, and when even Quakers could prophesy the downfall of all royal authority.

Guert Ten Eyck, away out on the Sound, was having a curious time. It was a splendid sail. It had been and still was full of excitement. The peril of it was by no means over, although not a sail was in sight, and the *Noank* was running fast before a favoring breeze. Guert, however, was conscious of having yet another new experience. He had had some schooling. His mother was a woman of education, moreover, and she had taught him many things. He had even read a number of books and he thought he knew a great deal. Now, he hardly knew how, he had been drawn to sit down by Nathan Hale, whom he knew to be a college graduate and a school teacher, and to tell him all he had learned, and to see how little there was of it, and then, as his handsome friend talked on, he began to feel a great, vague hunger to know more.

It was curious, that anything like a sea-lecture on knowledge should follow so closely upon the roar of the *Merlin's* guns, but there never could have been a time when all Guert's mind would be more completely awake. Besides, he was not talking to an ordinary man, and he was made to feel strongly the force of Nathan Hale's last remark:

"Read, Guert. Study. You will soon be called to act. Every American boy owes it to his country to be all the man there is in him. Anyhow, we are safe, now. It is getting dark."

Mrs. Ten Eyck did not sleep as well as usual, that night, and it may be that some of her thoughts concerning her son were pretty nearly correct. None were much out of the way that imagined him also to be pretty wide awake, much of the time, for he kept his watch on deck with the sailors and he had difficulty in shutting his eyes when he went below. She was also right in picturing to her mind a swift schooner, cracking on all sail, and dashing almost recklessly along the shortest course toward New London. She was up early, next morning, and her first visitor was no other than Co-co, followed closely by Up-na-tan and bringing a fine string of blackfish, caught at the turn of the tide. Co-co's eyes, however, did not brighten over his fish half so much as they did when he assured her:

"Bes' kin' ob wind, all night, Missus Ten Eyck. Blow 'em right along. King ship nebber cotch 'em."

"Boy all right," added the red man. "Know he come back. Take heap 'calp, some day. Heap like him. So, so! Up-na-tan!"

Guert was apparently a recognized ally of those two adventurers, whether or not they regarded him as a promising young white pirate. They went to work in Mrs. Ten Eyck's cornfield, without further orders, and it was not long before she had more visitors. She had to give up her spinning-wheel that morning, and it was to quite a knot of listeners, in the parlor, that Aleck Hamilton brought a specially interesting batch of news.

Not only had Skipper Avery, of New London, escaped the press-gang, after upsetting their boat, but he was almost believed, by the military and naval officers and His Excellency, Governor Tryon, to have regained his schooner, as she had instantly set sail. Worst of all was their black suspicion connecting the *Noank* with a discovered theft of four barrels of gunpowder. She was sure to be captured, however, as the brig *Spitfire* had followed her, and the sixty-gun *Merlin* was known to be in her way.

"Guert's on board of her," burst from the lips of Maud Wolcott. "They can't catch her. I know they can't."

"That is what Co-co and Up-na-tan say," remarked Mrs. Ten Eyck. "Skipper Avery must know the Sound as well as they do."

"They ought to know," said Aleck, but Rachel Tarns turned upon him with :

"Let it be a lesson to thee, Alexander. Submit

thyself to thy good king. If thee ever steals any of his powder thee should know beforehand what thee is going to do with it."

"We are going to need all the powder we can get, some day," replied Aleck. "But I hope they won't catch the *Noank*."

"Thee bad boy!" said Rachel. "Thee has no sympathy for thy king. That wicked man Lyme Avery is a deserter, and thee should wish him to be catched and hanged."

"They may hang me some day" — but the young man, or rather boy, stopped there and turned to go, with a somewhat hasty performance of ceremony.

"Thee had better go," said Rachel, "before thee talks treason. Thee must not talk treason in my presence, and thee must not steal, but if ever thee needs to buy a few barrels of powder for thy duck-shooting thee can come to me for the money."

"Rachel Tarns!" exclaimed Mrs. Ten Eyck, but after her guests were gone, she went into her back room and took down from some hooks in the alcove, something that may have been suggested by the mention of duck-shooting. It was a fine, bell-muzzled fowling-piece, of the largest size. It was as tall as a middle-sized man. It had a flint-lock, of course, and was very heavy, but it looked as if it could throw large shot and a great many of them.

"Guert has not been old enough, nor strong enough,

yet," she said, " but they say he is a good marksman. I will get the best powder. Plenty of it. I think I will get buckshot. Perhaps I can buy a musket."

What could she want of buckshot, when the nearest hunting-ground for deer was at least twenty miles from the city?

That was a grand day for a sailing party and Guert made the most of it. The *Noank* was a fine seaboat, and the old harpooneer told him of rough seas and trying weather when she had carried him and the skipper stanchly in their search for whales. She had even out-sailed a pirate, among the West India Islands. Guert longed to tell him of his own piratical adventure, but he shut his mouth tight, and was true to Up-na-tan.

The wind held fresh and southerly, and the few sails they sighted had no danger in them, but none were approached too nearly. It was just as well that not too many people of any kind should afterward be able to say they had seen the *Noank*.

The sun went down, and through the long hours of the evening watch, Guert sat and talked with Nathan Hale, excepting when Skipper Avery spun yarns about his voyages, or told of the doings of Old Put in the French and Indian War. It was a great evening, but Guert at last went down to his bunk, thinking of his mother, and wishing he could tell her how really safe he was, and how splendidly he and the *Noank* had beaten the British cruisers. He slept better this time. He did not know how long it was before he was shaken up sharply, and heard a voice say :

" Come, Guert ! "

" Is this New London ? " asked he, eagerly, for he heard Skipper Avery, on deck, shouting :

" Lower the boat."

" No," said Nathan Hale ; " it's the cove beyond Noank Point, east of New London. We must put the powder ashore."

" Powder ? " exclaimed Guert, springing out, wide awake. " Of course. We must hide it. What'll the *Noank* do ? "

" She'll run into New London harbor, perhaps," said Hale. " But I think she is off for a cargo of Virginia tobacco, if she can get away. That brig may be hunting along shore for her."

" They won't catch her," said Guert, as he and his friend hurried on deck. " They'd never find her in here, in the dark."

It was pretty dark. The one boat of the *Noank* had been lowered, and Mrs. Avery was already in her, with the two Avery boys, and the harpooneer and another seaman at the oars. It was a whale-boat, and was well able to carry also the two heavy barrels which were quickly lowered with the help of tackle.

" No danger in them," said Guert, " so long as there's no fire around."

"Nobody can guess when or whar that powder'll be fired away," replied the old harpooneer. "Come right down, my boy."

Guert obeyed, and in a moment more he was sitting by Mrs. Avery. It was a short pull to a rude wooden pier, at the beach, and there were men with lanterns, waiting. So, he quickly discovered, was a two-horse farm wagon.

"It's goin' to our farm, away over among the Groton Hills," said Mrs. Avery. "This 'ere is Deacon Prentice's wagon — old Sam Prentice. He's a cousin o' mine, and he's real grit. Oh! but ain't he mad about their 'pressin' Lyme."

Guert heard a deep, hoarse voice, at the wagon, talking all sorts of treason against King George, and adding:

"Biggest luck in the world to git so much paowder. Last time I seen Old Put, he was 'most sick to think on it, how leetle we hed on hand. We'll land it daown inter the skipper's own cellar, and then he'd best clear for the Capes and the Potomac. It won't dew for old George's men to ketch him, jist naow. This 'ere'll blaow over 'fore he gits hum with his terbacker."

Guert waited, impatiently, feverishly, while the boat made another trip. He saw the barrels hoisted into Sam Prentice's wagon, followed by Mrs. Avery. The wagon started, the boat put off, with hearty good-by words all around, and then Nathan Hale said:

"Now, Guert, you and I must foot it to New London. From what Sam Prentice says, I think we shall start you back to New York with an errand. How would you like a long ride?"

"I can ride," almost shouted Guert. "I can ride anything. I'm ready."

So they two set out together, in the early dawn, and Nathan Hale said:

"I'm afraid it won't be long before we shall have to use some of that powder."

CHAPTER V.

DISPATCHES FROM BOSTON.

THE mere escape of Skipper Avery was not a matter of great importance, seeing how many Yankee sailors there were to be caught, but the actual taking of four barrels of the king's own gunpowder marked with his broad-arrow, was quite another affair. It seemed to mean that somebody was going to shoot a great deal and was getting ready for it. It was so very important, that the British officers, of all kinds, and Governor Tryon, decided to keep it as nearly a secret as possible, and hope that the schooner would be captured.

There was no danger that Up-na-tan, or Co-co, or Rachel Tarns, or Maud Wolcott, would bring "the authorities" any information, for they were all rebels together. As for Mrs. Ten Eyck, she went over to spend the evening at Mrs. Murray's, after spinning desperately until the last twists of carded wool that she had on hand gave out. Meantime the old bell-muzzled gun stood in the corner and watched her spin, looking all the while as if somebody had given him a new suit of oil and polish, and had put a brand-new flint in his lock-mouth, ready to strike fire on the first opportunity.

Co-co was restless, and left the cornfield in the middle of the afternoon to go down to Mom Van Boom's, remarking :

" Mebbe pore ole brack man fine out wot dem lobsters is up to. Feel right shore dey nebber cotch de schoonah."

Up-na-tan seemed to be having a sulky day, not a proud one. Not that he looked at all humble when he ate his supper in Mrs. Ten Eyck's kitchen. He ate it in gloomy silence, when it was put before him by the middle-aged Dutch woman who was serving as help at the farmhouse. He hardly seemed to see her, and it was just as well, for she was one of at least a dozen who worked there, turn by turn, and one was as another to the great chief, the last of the Manhattans, the owner of the whole island.

Co-co was very much at home wherever he might happen to be, but nobody knew exactly where Up-na-tan lived. Nobody had ever cared to know, but there was a vague impression that he had a wigwam among the worthless masses of rocks and the woods and bushes that lay toward the Bloomingdale road, in the middle of Manhattan Island. It was a wild, tangled bit of country, and wildcats had been killed there. Perhaps it did not now contain anything much wilder-looking than was Up-na-tan himself, when, a little before dusk, he stood upon one of the highest knobs of granite and looked out eastward, across the Harlem flats and marshes, toward the Sound. He had not arrived there by any road, but had come all the way from the Ten Eyck place across lots. He was far enough from any road, now, but he was entirely at home and could feel that nobody wanted to dispute with him the ownership of the spot he stood on.

"Chief heap glad," he muttered, as he looked. "Colony men got powder. Kill all lobster. Up-na-tan help. Go see Iroquois pretty soon."

If the next words he uttered were in any dialect of the red man, they ended with "So, so! Up-na-tan!" and a fierce, prolonged war-whoop. That being finished, he turned and went down the side of the knob with a springy, pantherish tread, and disappeared among dense thickets and ragged masses of rock. On he pushed, for a minute or so, and he was not following any path. It was a shadowy, deep hollow that he paused in, then, with close-growing trees overhead. At his feet lay a slab of stone that seemed to lean against two shoulders of the broken ledge, and to be overgrown with briers.

Without a word spoken, Up-na-tan very carefully lifted aside the prickly vines, but he must have been a giant in strength to have raised that stone as he did. That is, he tilted it back and stepped over it into a great crevice, that grew wider from its entrance, and for a dozen feet, and then was blocked by a rocky wall. The break in the ledge and the fallen rocks had made a kind of cave. There never is any other kind in granite. Almost all the great caves are in limestone or basalt.

"Up-na-tan house," he said, as he looked around. "Paleface no find him. Kidd no come. So, so! Up-na-tan!"

Anybody would have uttered some kind of exclamation on looking around in that place, for it was a curiosity shop. There were a few weapons, swords, pistols, muskets, all wrapped up with some care. There were blackened specimens of valuable silverware that only needed polishing to ornament an earl's dinner table. There were bags and bags that only gave a hint of what might be in them, when the Manhattan lifted one of them and threw it down again, as if to hear it chink. Then he did so with another, and the chink was not the same. There is a difference in the ringing of gold and of silver. He did not open any bag.

"Captain Kidd money," he said. "He come for bag some day. Find some here. Some on island. Up-na-tan wait."

If he had fished all the night before, and then worked all day in the cornfield, instead of spending any of the treasure he was guarding, it may have made him weary. At all events, he went and pulled back the stone, bringing it toward him over the opening between the rocks, like a door or a hatch. He was then securely shut in, and he lay down among the heaps of strange things on the stone floor of his cave, and went to sleep. No man on Manhattan Island slept in a darker bedroom, that night, than did the man who claimed to own it all.

About the middle of the following forenoon, a small group of men stood in front of the old tavern at the foot of Main Street, in the busy, yet sleepy town of New London. Several horses were hitched near them, and one of them remarked :

"Wall, Paul, ye kem in from Baws'n on the clean jump, ye did, but you won't hev to go on to New York. Nathan's fetched up a Dutch boy that kin take yer place, so's you kin go hum."

Guert's cruise in the *Noank* had evidently been told, and now Nathan Hale said of him :

"He is clear grit, Revere. Sam Prentice has brought in your sorrel racer for him, and your mount is a good one."

"I'll trust him, if you say so," replied the celebrated Boston messenger, who had been looking at Guert half-doubtfully. "Besides, Old Put's dispatches must be carried right back to Boston. I must take them to Sam Adams and Dr. Warren, myself."

"I'll take anything to Mr. Livingston," said Guert, delighted with the idea of going home at once, with something important to carry.

"Take these papers, then, Guert," said Revere. "Put them inside; under your belt — so. There — draw it tighter. Now they'll stay, no matter how hard you ride. Mount! Captain Ledyard," he added, "before he is off, have you anything more you wish to send to Livingston or to the New York Committee?"

"No, I haven't," said a pleasant-looking man, standing at the side of Nathan Hale. "It's of no use. Livingston couldn't send Putnam's message to the Iroquois chiefs. No messenger" —

"Yes, he could," exclaimed Guert. "I can get him one, right away. Old Indian. Hates King George worse than any white man could hate him."

"That's it," interrupted Sam Prentice. "I know boys. He's one on 'em. Cutest kind. Naow, Ledyard, gin him that there tokin from Old Put for the redskins."

Captain Ledyard handed Guert a small parcel to put in his pocket, remarking:

"That's for Livingston to send to the Iroquois. If you get into danger, burn it, if you can. You have all your directions for the way, and know what houses to stop at. They will give you fresh horses about every twenty miles, if you need them, but you can ride

HE WAS LIKE PAUL REVERE, CARRYING COMMITTEE DISPATCHES.

that critter thirty and not tire him. It's one Paul Revere left here last trip. If he doesn't throw you "—

"He can't," shouted Guert, feeling as if he were all one tingle, but old Sam Prentice seemed to toss him into the saddle.

His feet caught the stirrups, his hands caught the reins, the splendid sorrel under him curveted, whinnied, danced around a little, and then shot away up the street, with a long, easy stride, while Guert almost screamed with pride and exultation. He was riding as a Colony messenger. He was like Paul Revere, carrying Committee dispatches. He was in danger. He was a rebel. He was a kind of trooper. He was mounted on a racer, and he was riding home. Hurrah!

It was yet an hour before noon of that day, when a dignified woman, and a girl not altogether so dignified, stood together at the cluttered counter of MacReady's old bookstall, on Pearl Street, near Broadway. Before them, and on other counters, and on all the shelves, was a very much mixed collection of old books and new, but they seemed to be examining two or three of the oddest kind. One, that lay open, was illustrated with copper-plate engravings that were curiosities. Some looked like forts, and some were collections of cannon. Some had a mathematical look. They were decidedly uninteresting, but the lady said:

"Thee is right, Maud. I am glad thee found them."

"I know these are the very books, Rachel," said

Maud, with a flushed face. " Aleck said so. All about artillery and forts. Cavalry, too, and infantry. See, there's Vaubau's name, and all the others. Plans of battles."

" Roy MacReady," said Rachel, raising her voice, " did thee say sixteen shillings for these wicked books about killing men ? "

" Sixteen for that volume. A guinea for the other. Twelve shillings-six for the smaller volume. I bought them all of an officer of the garrison, last year."

" Thee did right," said Rachel. " I am glad thee came by them honestly. I will buy them from thee. See that thee send them to my house."

There was a quiet kind of laugh near her, and a friendly voice asked :

" Rachel, can you tell me what business Quakers have with books about war ?"

" Robert Livingston," replied Rachel, " thee is a very great fool with thy questions. I am a woman of peace, and I do my duty, to keep thee, or the king's officers, or thy wicked Committee, or any other foolish and ignorant persons, from knowing how to kill men with guns. Thee cannot borrow them, Robert, nor will I lend them to thy wicked Liberty Boys, nor to thy Committee."

The courteous-mannered patriot evidently knew Rachel Tarns, for he was laughing, but his curiosity was aroused, for he asked :

"Miss Maud, can they be for you? Or for Mrs. Murray?"

"Do let me tell, Rachel," pleaded Maud.

"Thee bad girl! It is thy fault," said Rachel. "Robert, has thee been drinking thy king's tea, as is thy duty?"

"Not a drop," he said.

"Ah," said Rachel. "Thee does not like tea. I will say only a word to thee about the books. A young friend of mine at the college, wishes to know more about mathematics. He will be much instructed by the contents of these volumes. He will also learn how dreadful war is, and will incline toward peace."

"I think so. I quite agree with you," said Livingston, but Rachel had paid for the military books, and seemed to wish to get away, for she almost whispered:

"Robert, Maud and I must go. Some of thy rebellious committee-men are waiting for thee. See that they talk no treason, nor thee either. Honor thy good king and his wise ministers."

She swept slowly away, and Maud went with her, exulting:

"O, Rachel! I'm so glad you are so rich. Now Aleck Hamilton can learn about making forts, and armies, and winning battles" —

"Thee must never go to war, Maud Wolcott," replied Rachel, "but if any bad men are coming against thee, it is right to build strong places for thee to hide in.''

"Yes,'' exclaimed Maud. "Good forts, and cannon to shoot back with, and to know just how. Aleck says Aaron Burr is studying all the while, and there are plenty of books for him at Newark and Princeton.''

"I will see to it that Alexander shall know more than Aaron,'' said Rachel positively. "It is well for all young men to store their minds with knowledge. It is well for thee also to avoid the sin of ignorance. Thee can spin and thee can weave. Can thee make a tent?''

"Why, no,'' said Maud, as they walked along Broadway. "I never thought of it.''

"Then thee had better think,'' said Rachel, "for if thee will read thy Bible, thee will find it telling thee 'to thy tents, O Israel.' I shall buy canvas, and I will have tents ready for many men.''

Maud was startled as she looked at the stern face of the excited Quakeress, there was so much war in it, and such a glow of patriotic courage.

"You're as good and as brave as you can be, Rachel,'' she said. "I can't make a tent, but I can roll cartridges. So can both my aunts, at Litchfield, and they are teaching the girls.''

They had a great many things to say which would have sounded like treason, in the ears of a stanch loyalist, like Jane De Lancey, but she was not there to hear. It was entirely natural, however, that Maud went over to Mrs. Ten Eyck's, that evening, to tell her about the books, and to keep her company, and to wonder, every now and then, whether or not Guert had safely reached New London. It would have done them good if they could have known, then, and all the next few days, how very safely he got there, and how short a visit he made.

He rode out of New London, westerly, in high spirits, but with one piece of advice ringing in his ears.

"My boy," he had been told by Paul Revere, the Boston messenger, "one good reason why I let you go is that I'm told they might stop me. They've no right to. It's against all law, but they don't care much for that. Now, you'd best not talk much, nor ride along with anybody, but if you are followed, just let that horse go. They won't catch him."

Guert hoped, in his heart, that somebody would really give him a good excuse for letting out the speed that was in that sorrel, but for that day, at least, he was to be entirely disappointed. Nothing could have been more entirely peaceful than the manner in which he traveled. The roads were good, at that season, although they seemed to have been planned to go over all the hills instead of through all the valleys. Even Paul Revere's sorrel knew that it was best to walk up a hill, and then to walk down on the other side, but he loved to stretch out a little on anything like a level.

Guert had a luncheon with him, to eat half-way, while the sorrel nibbled grass and looked at him as if he were saying:

"You're not exactly a Boston boy, but I'll be good to you. Neither of us belongs to the king, and this isn't his grass, either."

Guert made no audible reply, but at that hour, Skipper Avery, standing on a wharf in New London Harbor, was remarking:

"All right, Captain Ledyard. It's goin' to be clear weather. We'll run the *Noank* in here, soon's it's dark. If the cargo's ready, we can stow her in two days and nights. If that brig doesn't look in, we're safe. We won't come back, right away, either."

But away down at the Battery, in New York, a knot of British officers, in uniform, were discussing the bad conduct of that very schooner.

"Do you think you winged her, captain?"

"I almost fear we did not. I couldn't risk losing the *Merlin* on those shoals, but the schooner seemed to slip over them."

"The brig may find her" —

"She signaled me she would put in at New Haven, and all along shore."

"That's right. She'll get her," said another officer wisely, but Skipper Avery's next voyage was all the safer because his enemy was hunting for him everywhere, so carefully, and losing time.

Guert mounted, and again rode on, now and then exchanging friendly greetings with country people. Not one of them was willing to let him go without getting all his news out of him, and he almost laughed aloud several times, as he said, at parting :

"Mister, I haven't met a man yet, nor a woman, that didn't agree about the right way to make tea. All the Connecticut people think salt water is best for it."

He felt very much as if he were among friends, but, as the afternoon passed, and the sorrel took things easier and easier, he found himself studying more closely the farmhouse dooryards.

"Haven't seen it yet," he said, at about six o'clock. "I must have passed more than one of them."

A minute later he gave a shout that startled the sorrel, and exclaimed :

"There it is ! The gate's open. I'll ride right in and get down."

There it was. Nothing but a coonskin nailed, head downward, against the bark of a tree, and Guert broke off a small branch from a bough of that tree before he dismounted. A woman came hurriedly down from the porch, and, as he handed her the twig, she said :

"Sech a boy, too ! Come right in. They'll keer for yer hoss. Ye must be right-down tired. Oh ! but ain't ye welcome, though. My name's Hannah Taber. Walk in."

She knew how to talk, but she and some other women, and some men and boys, knew also how to make him talk.

It was a big, hearty-voiced man who said .

"You've done first-rate. Thirty-odd mile, as the crow flies, and I don't know how many by the roads. You'll sleep. Prime good hoss, too. You could hev another in the mornin', if you needed one, but you won't. That's Paul Revere's thorrerbred. I knowed him when ye kem up the east road."

There was great talk, and much news-telling in that farmhouse, during the evening. Guert told all he knew, but he learned a great deal.

Before he went to bed, his mind was full of the great fact that all the American colonies of Great Britain were beginning to consult, and were getting ready to act as one people. He also knew that the British Government was anxious to know what the Colonies pro posed to do, and would be very glad to get hold of a lot of written dispatches such as were carried by Paul Revere and that very important horseman, Guert Ten Eyck. He went to sleep, saying to himself :

"I don't want to ride any other horse but the sorrel. I'll take good care of him, and make him carry me through."

That was a good enough idea, but when he and the sorrel were led out into the front yard, next morning, Paul Revere's fast horse seemed inclined to dance a little, while every muscle of Guert's body told him that he had ridden his longest ride, the day before, and had no dance in him.

As soon as he was well shaken into the saddle, the soreness disappeared, and he could enjoy his ride through the country, but there was only riding to do, for nobody seemed to have any idea of stopping him. It almost hurt his pride to be so entirely safe, but he was all the while growing impatient, and he could think a great deal about his mother and her anxiety over his absence.

Very early that morning, in a dense thicket of trees and briers, among the ruggedest rocks of Manhattan Island, a tall fellow was curiously busy arranging rubbish and trailing vines over a slanting stone. When he finished, it all looked natural, as if it had grown there, and he remarked :

"Ugh ! Lobster no find Kidd money. No find heap money in sand on seashore. Up-na-tan 'pend him all, some day. Not now."

He went stealthily out through the underbrush, with other mutterings, that told how well he understood the matter. If a more than suspected old pirate like himself were found spending money he could not account for, the authorities, particularly the red-coated "lobsters" whom he hated, would at once hunt for his treasure-house, and would be very likely to find it. He could content himself, therefore, with merely owning it, just as he owned the island it was hidden in.

That was a dull day for Mrs. Ten Eyck. So were some that followed it. They would have been duller, if it had not been for the manner in which her neighbors came to see her, and to tell her the news and ask if she had heard from Guert. Co-co and Up-na-tan stuck by the farm faithfully, but neither of them asked a question. The spinning-wheel had fresh supplies, and that and the loom were as great a help as was even Maud or Rachel. Aleck Hamilton came only once. It was his college vacation time, but he had hardly an hour to spare from some intensely interesting books procured for him by Maud and the Quakeress.

"Alexander," Rachel had said to him, "thee is a bad boy. Thee is not a Friend, and I do not wish thee to change thy views at this time. Thy country — I mean thy good and wise king — does not need any more Quakers. Learn all thee can, Alexander, for thee knows very little."

"I'll learn all there is in them," said young Hamilton feverishly, as he thanked her for the books. "I won't let Aaron Burr get ahead of me. He says he knows, now, how to handle a regiment, but I don't believe he knows how to handle artillery."

All that Guert was learning, during those days, was about the country along the coast of the Sound, and about horseback work as a messenger. Well, yes —

he learned that there were many devoted friends of King George scattered among the angry New England people, so that it was well for him to keep his errand to himself.

Dull — dull — dull — everybody in the city of New York said so, but it was largely because they were all waiting for something, for all the patriots were really in a kind of ferment, expecting great news from England, and from the Southern Colonies and from Boston. There were rumors of all sorts, and Governor Tryon and his council held as many meetings as did what they called the " rebel " Committee of Fifty-one or the Liberty Boys.

It was early on the morning of the sixth of July, 1774, that Mrs. Ten Eyck stood in the porch of her house, sadly and wearily shaking her head in reply to Maud's doleful question:

" Hasn't Guert come home? "

They were startled, just then. Past the house, with a springing, panther step, went Up-na-tan, sending out, as he went, a shrill, triumphant war-whoop.

Closely following him, with a strange agility for even an Ashantee with so white a head, went Co-co, shouting:

" Yo, yo, yo! — oh! Dat Guert! Yo! Stole a hoss an' fotch him along."

Mrs. Ten Eyck and Maud were at the gate therefore, wild, rejoicing, breathless, when a very proud-looking young rider pulled in a beautiful sorrel steed, to shout: "Mother! Maud! I can't wait now. I'm a Boston messenger. I must ride to Counsellor Livingston's. This is Paul Revere's own horse."

"O, Guert!" said his mother. "Come back as soon as you can."

"Hurrah!" was all Maud could think of, at the moment, while the Manhattan and the Ashantee uttered exultant yells, as the happy messenger waved his hand to them, and rode away.

Within an hour after that, it seemed as if something had suddenly stirred up all the people on Manhattan Island.

Men rode and ran, this way, that way, or met in knots on the streets, in the shops, in the houses. The Governor called his council together. The British garrison of Fort George received strict orders to keep in quarters, for fear of trouble. Loyal servants of the king could hardly express their indignation, for a great meeting had been called to assemble on the Common, and carpenters were putting up a platform.

Guert spent most of his day at home, telling all his news over and over again, but there were some things he could not tell, even to his mother or her friends.

He had a long talk with Co-co and the Manhattan, before dinner time. That is, he talked, and they listened, but at the end of it, Co-co shook his head and said:

"Nebber do. Guert 'tay at home. He not'ing to do in de woods. Injin business!"

"Ugh!" said the latter. "Boy heap fool. Up-na-tan go. See all Six Nation. No let Sir William Johnson know. No let Thay-en-dan-e-ga hear. No let Six Nation fight Colony. Ready go now!"

"That's all I want," said Guert, and not a great while afterward he went down town.

The crowd was already gathering on the Common, and before six o'clock it was the greatest public meeting yet held on Manhattan Island. Then the leading citizens on the platform called for order, named a chairman and other officers, and then were read, loudly, clearly, that all might hear, dispatches from the patriot legislature of Massachusetts, advising New York and the other Colonies to choose delegates to a Continental Congress, to be held in Philadelphia.

It was a startling piece of advice, and two or three speakers who discussed it first, were disposed to handle it gingerly.

"I'll speak, Aaron Burr. I will"—exclaimed an eager-toned voice, near Guert, in the crowd, and then there was a pushing through, and a slight, graceful form sprang upon the platform.

"Collegian! collegian!" shouted derisive voices, as the crowd heard a shrill "Mr. Chairman!" and it was half a minute before silence came. Pretty quickly afterward, there was astonishment and then enthusiasm, for the best, bravest, most eloquent argument in favor of a union of the Colonies against the king and his ministers, was made by a boy of seventeen.

"Isn't it great, Aaron?" exclaimed Guert.

"I'm a year older than Aleck Hamilton," said Burr. "I can do as much as he can. I'm off for Newark and Princeton."

"I'm only fourteen," said Guert to himself. "I brought the dispatches, anyhow. I wish Up-na-tan would let me go with him among the Iroquois."

CHAPTER VI.

THE NEWS FROM LEXINGTON.

PAUL REVERE'S sorrel was in Mrs. Ten Eyck's barn. He did not seem any the worse for his journey, and Co-co undertook the task of "shining him up" as if he loved him.

"Guert," said a member of the Committee, after thanking him heartily, "take good care of that sorrel. Revere will ride him back, next time he comes. He may only take him as far as New London, but he has made the through trip on him, more than once."

"Oh! that's it," said Guert. "He knew all the roads, and he knew what houses to stop at. I believe he knew the people, too."

Very likely he did, but Guert's first errand, on the morning of July 5, 1774, brought him and Up-na-tan to the barn in the rear of the Livingston mansion, for a talk with the learned and patriotic man who was to be one of the New York representatives in the Continental Congress. He was there waiting for them, and he seemed to know the Manhattan pretty well already. Many things had been discussed between them when Guert brought him the Boston dispatches, on the fourth. His idea now, as it seemed to Guert, was to find out whether he could trust Up-na-tan, and whether it was worth while to try him. Perhaps the red man saw it as Guert did, for he said after a thoughtful silence :

"Send pale face, send nigger, no good. Send Manhattan. Indian talk with Indian. Stay a heap. Wait. Hear. Talk. See ole friend. Know all Iroquois chief. Thay-en-dan-e-ga heap bad snake. Johnson heap king man — Up-na-tan hate king."

"What for?" quietly asked Livingston.

"Look!" suddenly exclaimed the last of the Manhattans, drawing himself up proudly. "You heap chief, like Up-na-tan. Navy men 'press Livingston, eh? Keep him whole year 'fore he 'cape? Flog, eh? Kick, eh? Make slave of Livingston? How he feel? Feel good? Ugh! Talk no. So, so! Up-na-tan!"

"I'm glad you got away," exclaimed Livingston. "I'll trust you. You are just the man we want. There isn't any danger that a flogged Indian will forgive. That'll do, Guert. Up-na-tan, your message will be ready at sunset."

"Come," said Up-na-tan, and he and his young friend went off together.

There was hardly any other political or military

question that promised to be of greater importance to the patriots of the British province of New York, in any struggle with the king, than would be the course of the powerful Iroquois confederacy. If all the tribes between the Hudson and the great lakes should be united as a re-enforcement of the British troops, it seemed as if the colonists would have no hope at all. Guert was well aware of it, and it did him good all over to think that he was helping to keep the red-skins from joining the men in red uniforms. He had found, however, that it was of no use for him to plead, especially with his mother, for permission to go with Up-na-tan upon his secret mission. The latter, indeed, had replied with little more than:

"Ugh! Heap boy!"

Just now, however, he was altogether silent, as he led the way. Not one of Guert's questions would he answer, as they went over fence after fence and across farm after farm. He went rapidly, too, and his face grew fiercely gloomy, as if his thoughts might be of a pretty dark kind. Right on, into the great, rocky barren where nobody lived or could get a living, but where, as Guert knew, Up-na-tan was supposed to sometimes set up his wigwam. Everybody knew that there was no house there; not even a hut.

At last they went up and over a high, knobby ledge, and Guert still saw no wigwam. Neither did he know that he had nearly reached the lair of his savage friend, not even when he went down with him into the briery hollow beyond.

"Guert look," said Up-na-tan, pointing at the slanting stone. "Make heap big promise to Up-na-tan."

"I'll promise," said Guert. "What is it — that stone?"

"Count," said the Indian. "Count summer. Guert only fourteen summer. Mark on stone. Take small stone."

He spoke slowly, and much more clearly than usual, and Guert obeyed, making marks on the flat slab until he said "Twenty-one."

"One week, seben," said the Indian. "Two week, fourteen. Three week, twenty-one. Mebbe Up-na-tan lose 'calp. Mebbe Huron take 'em. Mebbe Iroquois. Lose 'calp sometime, anyhow. Mebbe lobster shoot, hang, kill. Mean to kill heap lobster. Up-na-tan dead. Guert twenty-one. Come take up 'tone. See what find. Keep promise?"

Guert promised, and Up-na-tan added:

"When take up 'tone, Guert know heap. No tell den. Take up 'tone now, lose hair. T'roat cut. Knife come. Boy die. So, so! Up-na-tan!"

Guert shuddered, but he had no thought of breaking faith, and was glad enough to get away from a place which contained so very dangerous a mystery. At the top of the ledge Up-na-tan paused, and pointed toward the Ten Eyck place.

"No come look at 'tone till three week make twenty-one summer," he said, and while Guert made his way homeward, the Manhattan wheeled, and strode off through the tangled woodland.

Guert did not hurry home, but he reached it only to find something that was not at all romantic. It was Rachel Tarns.

"Thee lazy, bad boy," she said. "Did thee hear Alexander speak, at the meeting?"

"I heard him," began Guert. "Aaron Burr and I" —

"Stop thee talking," said Rachel. "Thee will never speak at any meeting. Thee does not know anything. Why will not thee be of some use to thy country — to thy king? Thee is not old enough, yet, but thee can study, and thee can grow up" —

Maud had come with Rachel and she interrupted her there, with:

"O, Rachel Tarns! Guert did do something. He brought the dispatches all the way from New London, and they said the horse came all the faster because he had only a boy to carry."

"I know that," said Rachel. "It was Paul Revere's horse, and it should be hung for treason. The wicked beast! But if Guert will study the books I will give him, for bringing that horse safe to New York, he will be worth more to his country, for he will have a country of his own before many days. Will thee study for thy country, Guert, if I give thee the books?"

"I will," said Guert heartily.

"Then I will tell thee," she said. "Thee may come and get them at my house. Thee must know the testimony concerning thy country. There will be no king there, and thee may serve God in thine own way. Then if thee is a Quaker, thee will not be put in prison for it, nor hanged, nor burned. Neither will thee be burned nor drowned for any other faith, nor because they call thee a witch."

"What do you mean, Rachel?" demanded Mrs. Ten Eyck, in astonishment.

"What do I mean?" said Rachel. "Why does any Quaker think well of liberty? Is thee free, now? Is thy son free? I will tell thee a thing. Has thee a family tree — father, mother, grandfather, grandmother? So have I, and if I follow mine back, I find one road ends in fire at a stake, another at a gibbet, another in the water, another in a dungeon. Every one of them, man or woman, died for their free faith."

"Guert," exclaimed his mother, "get the books. Read! Study! Learn all you can! Grow up fast! I'll let you be a soldier. I'd rather you died in battle, a hundred times, than not have you free."

The face of Rachel Tarns was grand to look at, as she slowly, steadily, said:

"My grandmother was burned to ashes. She was

a Friend, and she could not fight, but I tell thee — for I was named after her — that old Rachel Tarns, the Quaker witch of York, died bravely in battle. So shall this land become free if its men shall prove as brave as its women."

"Oh!" exclaimed Maud. "I'm glad the boys are ready to fight. The girls are."

"All the boys I know are ready to do anything," said Guert, "but there isn't anything to do, yet."

That is, there was no fighting, and it was not easy to guess how very much was going on. There were no telegraphs, no newspapers of any account, nothing but talk and letter-writing, to spread news with. Even letters could not go often, and were very slow in going. Still, there was really a great deal done, whether people knew it or not, and day after day, the country was getting ready for something that was to come.

Rachel Tarns had told Guert that he must get himself ready, and he was almost astonished at the way he worked at books, during the remainder of that summer. Then he was almost disgusted, for several times while he was at home, reading in one room, while his mother was spinning or weaving in the other, Maud Wolcott came in to tell of exciting things which had occurred down in the busy part of the city. There were riots of all kinds. There were fights between the red-coated lobsters and the Liberty Boys, which sounded to Guert like battles, and he was not in one of them. It was pretty hard to bear, but it did him good to know that Aleck Hamilton was shut up with another lot of books.

"His are all about war," said Guert to Maud. "He'll know about armies and guns and forts."

"He means to be a general, some day," replied Maud. "So does Aaron Burr. Do you know what he did?"

"He hasn't been at our house," said Guert.

"He came to Mrs. Murray's," said Maud, "and told her what he wanted, and she let him have a horse, and he has been through every road and street and path, all over the island, away up to Harlem and Spuyten Duyvil Creek, and over in Westchester. He made maps, too. Aleck showed me some maps that he himself made" —

"I see," exclaimed Guert. "If there's ever a war on Manhattan Island, they'd know where to march. But then Co-co and Up-na-tan know more than any map. I know every corner of this island. Wish I knew what has become of Up-na-tan."

"Oh! wouldn't I," said Maud, but neither of them could have imagined precisely how much they would have had to know or see.

If they had been with the last of the Manhattans, that summer, and on into the autumn, they might have visited the great fort at Ticonderoga, on Lake Champlain, that was once French and now was British, and would soon be American. They might have gone up

Lake George in a canoe, and then have visited the great Johnson mansion, in the wilderness. Then they might have gone up the Mohawk Valley, and on to the Oneida Stone, to attend a council of that tribe. They would, surely, have seen the great council of the Iroquois, at the Sacred Fire of the Onondagas, the fire that never went out till the Six Nations were broken. Up-na-tan was there at the Succotash feast, where the white dog was burned, and he went on to the Senecas and to the Cayugas and southward to the Tuscaroras, and everywhere he heard and saw a great deal that no white messenger could have heard or seen. Besides, if Guert had gone with him, as he said:

"Boy lose hundred 'calp. No go home. Iroquois worse than lobster. Heap kill."

When he made that remark he was lying among some bushes, near the edge of a great precipice. The leaves around and above him were red and yellow, for the October days had come. The great chasm before him was full of mist, and of a vast roar of plunging sound, through which Up-na-tan stared gloomily at a wonder of falling water, for his long scout among the Iroquois had brought him to Niagara.

"Seneca no find him," he muttered. "Up-na-tan see Great Spirit Water. Now go home. Know heap."

Guert, too, had been almost thinking that he had learned enough from his books, that day, but when he put them down it was to go away from home. He went to Mrs. Murray's, and as he walked up the carriage way, he saw that the piazza contained quite a group of women, older and younger. Hardly was his hat off, moreover, before one of them stepped forward and said to him:

"Guert, thee bad boy, has thee heard the news? Thy good king is taking away from thee all the soldiers in thy fort and is sending them to Boston."

"We can get along without 'em," somewhat bluntly responded Guert.

"Could thee?" said Rachel sarcastically. "But what if he should take away thy good governor? There is said to be danger of even that. What would thee do then, thee poor boy?"

"Get along without him," replied Guert, with an emphasis which seemed to produce a sensation on the piazza.

"Could thee, indeed?" came very crisply from the unusually stern Quakeress. "Thee is very presumptuous, Guert. Thee does not know what dreadful things may be before thee. What if thy good king should cast thee off, and have no more to do with thee and thy wicked city? What could thee do?"

"Get along without him," said Guert, more sturdily than ever; but an angry voice behind Rachel exclaimed:

"Treason! What are we coming to? What? Get along without any king?"

"Jane," said Rachel, "thee does it all the while.

Thee has never seen George, in thy life, and thee keeps thy health finely. But thee is out of tea now, and thee cannot buy any more."

"Guert," said Maud, leaning over the piazza railing, "it's true. There will hardly any soldiers be left here. They are all going to Boston."

"I guess what's left will stay in the fort, then," said Guert. "So much the better for the Liberty Boys."

"The king's troops may go," said Miss De Lancey, with a sincerity as deep as Rachel's own, "but they will come again. They will hold this town, too, and every De Lancey will be with them."

"Thee is a good woman, Jane," remarked Rachel. "I like to hear thee speak thy mind and bear thy testimony" —

"They will put down treason in Boston," said Miss De Lancey, "and then they will come and put it down here."

"Perhaps they will," said Guert, "but it'll take a good many of 'em."

"Thee must not talk treason, Guert," said Rachel. "Thee may wear a red coat thyself, some day."

It seemed to be a new idea to Guert, and his face flushed, suddenly. It was as if an answer sprang to his lips.

"Mother says I'm to be a soldier," he said, "but Aleck Hamilton says we can't wear red. He thinks our uniform will be a kind of blue, to tell the troops apart, in a fight."

"Go home, thee bad boy!" exclaimed Rachel, as a kind of uproar began among the other women. "Tell thy mother I am coming to talk with her about thee" —

"I'll go to the gate with you," said Maud, springing down the steps. "The New England men wore blue at the siege of Louisburg" —

Guert saw that both Rachel and Mrs. Murray wanted him to go, before his too free tongue should stir up any more trouble, and he went.

"O, Guert!" said Maud, "I wish you were a foot taller. Aleck, too. As tall as that splendid Nathan Hale."

"I'm growing," said Guert, and then she told him all the rest of the news, to carry to his mother.

New York was indeed left with a slender garrison, during all that following winter. Warships came and went, but the military and naval center of British operations in America was the port of Boston. There had been no actual fighting there, as yet, but all the news from Massachusetts and the other New England colonies was stormy. So was much that came from the South, and from Congress, and all that came from England was full of threats. The worst tidings of all came every now and then from the Indian frontiers, for nowhere were the red men really at peace, and their dealings with some of the more exposed settlers were like an awful warning of terrible things to come.

Guert kept his promise to Up-na-tan about the stone, saying to himself:

"Just as likely as not he has been killed, but I've no right to touch it till I'm twenty-one. He's been gone an awful long time. So has Co-co."

That strange, old black man went up the Hudson in a sloop, just before the river froze over, and could hardly be expected back until spring; but there were not many inquiries concerning him.

It seemed as if the people of New York were becoming very good in the spring of 1775, they all went to church so regularly. The churches were down town, and on Sundays the houses up the island must have been almost deserted. Nobody was willing to miss hearing the preaching or anything else that there might be to hear, for news was likely to come at any hour.

There was nothing unusual, therefore, in the fact that, on the morning of April 22d, the Bowery Lane, and the streets it led into, and Broadway were all alive, just as the bells were ringing their best.

Guert and his mother had reached the corner of Broadway, opposite St. Paul's, and Mrs. Murray's carriage had caught up with them, just as a great shouting began to rise along the Bowery. Everybody else was looking, and they looked, but in an instant Guert himself shouted:

"Courier from Boston! That's old Sam Prentice's gray mare. I know her. She carried Paul Revere, once."

It was indeed a man who rode a gray steed, wet with perspiration, and who galloped with frequent pauses, reining in by group after group to shout with trumpet voice some news that came for all.

In a few minutes more, he was pouring out his tidings to a swiftly-gathering throng at the Broadway corner, and every time he paused for breath his gray mare curveted under him joyously, and the hats of men were waved in the air, and the handkerchiefs of excited women. The air was full of exultant exclamations.

"Lexington! Concord! British defeated! Colonel Smith! Lord Percy! General Gage! The farmers drove 'em to Boston! Hurrah for the Massachusetts militia! The war's begun!"

Through all, there suddenly came, from behind Guert, a shrill, fierce, penetrating whoop, prolonged, repeated, and at the end of it:

"Ugh! Boston men kill a heap! Whoop! So, so! Up-na-tan! Cayuga 'calp!"

"Yo, yo, yo!" came in a mellower tone, triumphantly, as the ferocious-looking Manhattan drew from a small bag and swung in the air, what seemed at least a half-dozen of the fearful trophies of savage victory.

"Thay-en-dan-e-ga send heap fool on trail of Up-na-tan. Whoop!"

"GUERT, THAT WAS YOUR FATHER'S GUN."

"Yo, yo! Co-co take four;" and the Ashantee waved his own trophies as proudly as did the red pirate beside him.

The Boston messenger saw and shuddered, but he said to Counsellor Livingston:

"That's something for me to tell when I get back. We heard they were going to come out for the king."

Again he shouted his own news, while all who were near the Manhattan and Co-co, crowded closer to question them.

"Alexander?" came from Mrs. Murray's carriage. "What is thee waiting for, now? Thee told me thy men were only waiting for the king's guns in the City Hall. Now is thy time."

"Hurrah! The City Hall!" answered a kind of general roar, as young Hamilton sprang away, followed by a score of vigorous fellows who took an evident pride in forming by fours, as they went.

"Those are some of the men he has been drilling," said Maud to Mrs. Murray. "He will have his cannon, now."

"And Rachel Tarns has paid all the expense of fitting out his company," replied Mrs. Murray. "What a fighting Quaker she is!"

"Guert? Guert? The *Noank* is down at the Albany pier" —

"Skipper Avery?" eagerly responded Guert, turning to another arrival.

"Why—you here?"

"Been here three days. Been down the coast. But I saw those two ships with supplies for the red-coats at Boston," said the skipper hurriedly. "They'll be setting sail if we're not quick about it. Get all the men you can. We must take them before they hear this Lexington news"—

"So, so! Up-na-tan!" and again the war-whoop sounded, and he and Co-co did more than Guert could, or the skipper, to summon helping hands for a possible sea-fight, as they all set off down Broadway.

"Yo, yo, yo!" yelled the Ashantee.

"Board 'em! Board 'em!"

"Maud," said Mrs. Murray, "don't lean out so far, you will fall."

"No, I won't," shouted Maud. "Mrs. Murray? Rachel Tarns? I heard him! Guert is leading those men to capture the two supply ships. They'll get them; I know they will. I want to see it."

"Go, go!" said Rachel. "Sarah Murray, tell thy driver. Anneke Ten Eyck, come and get in. Come and see thy boy help those wicked men take the ships of thy king. Alexander has gone to get his guns."

It was a time of wild excitement, and the fat, heavy carriage horses actually trotted fast as they were urged down Broadway, and out through dusty side streets, to the foot of Whitehall slip.

"There they go," said Maud. "Guert is in the first boat. Co-co and Up-na-tan are with him."

So were as many more as one boat could safely carry, and another, a whaleboat, crowded with stalwart fellows, was just pulling away from a schooner which lay at the next wharf. Out in the stream lay a handsome bark, and a medium-sized, full-rigged merchantman, both evidently well laden, even to their deck cargoes of hay for the cavalry and artillery horses of General Gage's troops, defending Boston from the rebels and colonists.

There was not one British man-of-war in the harbor to interfere with the fierce rush of the New York boys, older and younger. There were minutes of swift rowing, and then there arose once more the war-whoop of the Manhattan, as he sprang over the bulwarks of the bark. It was answered from the other vessel by the stentorian lungs of Skipper Avery, shouting:

"Hurrah for Lexington! Hurrah for old Connecticut! Hurrah for Liberty!"

At the Whitehall wharf stood a girl, swinging her handkerchief and crying, "Hurrah!" choked as she tried to say it, but Rachel Tarns, in the carriage behind her, stood up calm and dignified, as she remarked:

"None of King George's horses will get any of that hay."

There were no stores for King George's army or navy left upon either of those ships. The crews had not attempted any resistance, almost to the disgust of Co-co and Up-na-tan, but the *Noank* was shortly alongside to take off quite a cargo for New London.

There had been even a greater success on shore, for Governor Tryon was in England, and the officer in command of the fort had no force worth sending out to interfere with the Liberty Boys, minute-men and militia companies that were parading up and down Broadway. If services went on in any of the churches, after the bells ceased ringing for the news from Lexington, the congregations were but thin. It was late in the day when Guert reached home, and when he did so, his mother met him in the porch, holding out something. Her face was white, but she said :

"Guert, that was your father's gun. He carried it in the old French War. You can have it now."

CHAPTER VII.

THE GREAT CHIEF AND UP-NA-TAN.

GUERT TEN EYCK had a great deal of thinking to do concerning the fight at Lexington between the Massachusetts farmers and the soldiers of King George.

"There's just such another fight ready to come, right here," he said to Maud Wolcott.

"That's what Aunt Murray thinks," replied Maud; "but in Connecticut, you know, we haven't any red-coats to fight with; not many Tories, either."

"They're the worst of it," said Guert. "We might have to shoot real good fellows, like Steve De Lancey. Seems to me, I'd hate to shoot anybody I know."

"Well, maybe they've as good a right to their opinions as we have to ours," said Maud doubtfully. "I don't see how they have, for we're right and they're wrong."

"They've got the king on their side, anyhow,"

said Guert, "and all the lobsters, and all the ships of war, and all the Indians — Up-na-tan says. He knows all about 'em."

"I don't care," exclaimed Maud. "We're right."

There had been news from New London, and Guert knew that his friend Nathan Hale was a soldier under General Putnam.

"He'll make a good one," he said to Maud; "but I wish I knew what Skipper Avery is going to do with the *Noank*. He said she'd make a good privateer. There's lots of powder for it in those four barrels, but he doesn't know where to get any cannon."

"I hope he'll get some," said Maud; "but we want bigger ships than that schooner is."

"We can't get any now, though," responded Guert, "and the *Asia* and the rest of 'em in the harbor can shoot right into all the lower wards. It's the meanest place to live in."

That might be, but commerce seemed to be active, and the merchants were making money. Some of them were also said to be sending their wealth to England, to put it out of harm's way.

"I don't know who'd steal it," said Guert to his mother, when he told her about it; "but the folks in Boston are worse off than we are. What if we had a lot of lobsters quartered at our house, and had to live with 'em!"

"If we did, I'd leave the house and the city, too,"

said Mrs. Ten Eyck. "I don't much care to stay here if Governor Tryon is to come back and put us down."

That was what Royalists like the De Lanceys were waiting for, and, meantime, they would hardly speak or visit with their neighbors who supported Congress. Mrs. Ten Eyck, on the other hand, had never before had so many visitors, and perhaps it was because people could talk right out, at her house, especially if they were like Rachel Tarns when she said:

"Anneke, it does me so much good to come and talk treason with thee."

No doubt that was why there were so many at Mrs. Ten Eyck's on the morning of June 20, 1775. There were no men, to be sure, for they were all down town, but there were older and younger women, and not one of them seemed to want to sit still. They were in the house and out of the house, and some talked a great deal, and some were very sober and silent.

"Guert," said Maud, "did you hear that? They say some of Prescott's men at Bunker Hill were nothing but boys."

"Don't I wish I'd been there!" replied Guert. "If we ever have a fight in New York, I'm going to be in it."

Next to the great news of the battle at Boston, was the tidings that the Continental Congress had chosen Colonel Washington, of Virginia, to be Commander-in-chief of the American armies, and that he was coming through New York on his way to Massachusetts.

"I'm going to see him," exclaimed Maud. "He won't wear a red coat, I know."

"Thee may be sure of that," said Rachel; "but, Anneke, what is that boy of thine doing out there? I'll go and see. That gun is half a head taller than he is."

Out she went, into the side yard, followed by a small procession that seemed to be as heavily charged with Bunker Hill as was Guert himself, whatever he might have put into that wicked-looking old shooting-iron.

"Guert," exclaimed Rachel, "what is thee going to do? That gun is too big for thee."

"So it is," said Guert. "I never fired it off yet. Guess it would tire out me or almost anybody else to carry it far. But, don't you see? I can rest it over the stone wall, just as our folks did at Lexington, and I could blaze away. If it was a breastwork to shoot over, I could take as good aim as any of the boys did at Bunker Hill. I could hit 'em."

"Guert," said Maud, "let me try. Show me how. Why, how heavy it is! I can hardly lift it and lean it over the wall."

"That's it," said Guert. "Look along the sights, and point it at that chicken. He's just about as far off as the redcoats were when Putnam and Prescott told 'em to fire."

"I see him," she said. "He's the reddest feathered kind of chicken, too. He's a redcoat."

One of her eyes was shut tight, and the other was glancing excitedly along the barrel, just as she had seen Guert doing, and she did not know that he had cocked the gun. Neither, perhaps, did he, but she added:

"I could pull the trigger. I know I could."

Click — flash — bang — and there was a roaring report at that moment.

"Maud!" screamed Mrs. Ten Eyck.

"O, Maud!" gasped Guert, as he stooped and picked her up. "Did it hurt you?"

"Not a bit," said Maud, rubbing her shoulder, while they crowded around her. "But how it does kick. Guert, did I hit anything?"

Her answer came, loud and shrill, from a few yards beyond the wall; for the red-feathered fowl was walking away, strutting and crowing triumphantly.

"Maud," said Rachel, "thee should not shoot at the chickens that are on thy own side. There are no Tories in Anneke Ten Eyck's coop."

"I aimed right — I know I did; but I'm glad I didn't kill him," said Maud, as the excited rooster crowed again.

"The shot went too high because the gun kicked," said Guert. "I put in too much powder" —

"Anneke," said Rachel suddenly, "thee has another guest."

"O, Guert!" said Maud, looking, "it is Aaron Burr. Don't tell him about the chickens. He'll say girls can't shoot. He is always making fun of them."

"Here I am, Mrs. Ten Eyck," rang out at that moment, in front of the house. "I've come to see if Guert can tell me where I can find a good horse. I only borrowed this pony to carry me as far as Harlem."

"Aaron," came reprovingly in Rachel's voice, before Mrs. Ten Eyck could speak, "thee ought to be at Princeton over thy books."

"So my tutor said," replied Aaron, "but at last they let me get away. I'm going to join Old Put, if I have to travel the rest of the way on foot."

"That would take thee too long," said Rachel.

"I wish I was going," shouted Guert, all but angrily; but Rachel went on:

"I think Israel may need thee to do errands for him. Thee could be very useful, and thee should get there as soon as thee can. Thee had better go by my house on thy way. If thee is a rebel, thee is most likely a thief also. Thee had better steal thee a good saddle and horse from my stable."

"O, Rachel!" exclaimed Mrs. Ten Eyck, "that's just what I'd like to do."

"Anneke," said Rachel, "I know now why I was moved to buy that long-legged gray beast, when I had no use for her. Aaron, thee may steal her. If ever thee has to run away from thy enemies, she will out-run them."

"Maud," said Mrs. Murray excitedly, "run home! I'm just as loyal as Jane De Lancey is, but you may give Aaron that pair of silver-mounted holsters, and the pistols are in them. They are as good as new. There's a sword, too, in the closet behind my room."

"Aaron," shouted Maud, "come to Mrs. Murray's as soon as you steal the horse."

"Hurrah for Bunker Hill!" yelled Guert.

"Hurrah for Liberty!" shouted back Aaron, as he sprang upon his pony and dashed away.

"Thee get along, too," said Rachel to Maud. "I'm glad thee can do something. By and by thee will be putting in thy precious time in making cartridges" —

"That's what they are doing at home," said Maud, preparing to hurry away. "I wish I were there to help. Aaron will see them on his way, too."

"They don't need you," said Mrs. Murray, "and I do. You are all the home company I have. Besides, I can't let you neglect your books and your music. There'll be war soon enough, right here in New York."

"Guert," said Rachel, "put up thy big gun and go down to the Battery. Thy mother wants to know if there is any more news. See if the warships of thy king are coming in."

Maud was all excitement when she reached the Murray place.

"Aaron's nineteen," she said. "He's short for his age, but he'll want a sword and pistols if he's to ride on General Putnam's errands. Aunt Murray doesn't mean to give them to him herself. I s'pose she thinks they'd call it treason, and so I may give them."

It seemed hardly any time at all before she had been upstairs and was down again and out on the piazza. Mrs. Murray's husband was a Quaker if she was not, but here was her niece carrying in one hand a sheathed sword and its belt, and dragging with her other hand a heavy pair of holsters. She unbuckled one of these, and took out a long-barreled, handsomely made horse-pistol.

"How heavy it is," she said. "I couldn't aim a pistol as big as that is."

She put it back into its holster, and drew the sword out of its sheath. It was not a crooked, cavalry saber, but a long, straight, sharp-edged blade, with an ivory hilt and gilded guard. The blue steel was not bright and it did not glitter as she waved it, looking very warlike.

"I wonder if those spots are rust," she said, as she examined it more closely. "They are pretty red."

She was still studying the sword and wondering whether or not it had ever killed anybody, when

Aaron Burr came cantering up to the steps on Rachel's gray mare.

"Miss Wolcott," he said, laughing, "Rachel said I could run away fast enough. I guess I could. That's just what this gray wants to do. I can hardly hold her."

He could dismount and tie her, however, in spite of her objections, but while he was doing so his eager eyes were wandering to the array of weapons waiting for him on the piazza. He was in a perfect fever of delight when he sprang up the steps to take possession.

"Maud," he exclaimed, "is that the sword she meant to give me? She told me about it once. It's been in battles in Europe, and it went through Braddock's campaign. It's an old war sword."

"Then those spots may be blood," said Maud. "I do hope you won't ever really have to kill anybody."

"Yes, I will," said Aaron, and there came into his face a hard and pitiless look, as he took the sword in his right hand and sprang its elastic blade back and forth. "It's a soldier's business to kill or be killed. Now I must be off. I'm ready to ride with Old Put. There'll be hard fighting wherever he is."

His voice sounded harsh and vindictive, and Maud almost felt that she did not like him. He did not say a word while he strapped the holsters in front of his saddle, buckled the sword-belt around his waist, and untied the gray mare.

"I do like him, though," thought Maud. "He is going to be a soldier. He is brave, too. And how I do hope he won't be killed."

He sprang lightly into the saddle, but it was hard to hold in the gray. She gave him barely time to say:

"Thank you, Miss Wolcott. I shall see your family at Litchfield. Please tell Mrs. Murray how much I thank her. Oh! how I thank Rachel Tarns. Tell them they shall never be ashamed of Aaron Burr."

He was off; and Maud looked after him very thoughtfully, as she said:

"I can see it in his face. If he ever has to kill anybody, he won't hesitate a minute."

Guert went down town after news, as he was ordered, but he would much rather have gone with Aaron after the horse and weapons, and to talk about Old Put and Boston camps. He was all the more dissatisfied, therefore, when a long hunt gave him nothing to take home but what everybody knew before — that General Washington, or Mr. Washington, as all the Tories called him, was expected in a few days, and so was Governor Tryon, with a strong British fleet. The New York Congress, as the legislature was called, wanted Washington to come, but had no power to prevent Tryon also from landing, under the guns of a man-of-war.

"It wouldn't do to shoot him," said Guert to his

mother, "if he didn't do anything but come ashore and go to his own house."

He did not know how severely the leading patriots of New York were troubled on that very point; and one of their many talks was of some importance to him, and was taking place at the western gateway of the grounds of the Robert R. Livingston place. Only two American patriots were there, but they both represented the island pretty well.

"You wish to speak to General Washington when he comes?" said Livingston. "Well, I think you must do so. I will tell him at once, on his arrival. He will be glad to get your report direct."

"So," said the Manhattan. "Want talk with great chief. All Six Nation know him. Big fight, long ago. Tell him heap. So, so! Up-na-tan!"

"I will let you know," said Livingston.

"Good!" said Up-na-tan. "Bring Co-co. Bring boy Guert. Want big chief to see brack man. Want him see boy."

"Just as you please," said the thoughtful statesman, as Up-na-tan strode away; and he added: "It's of no use to ask him why. Best let him have his own way. I suppose Washington can get more out of him than I could, and he will know what to do with it, too. Congress did wisely in selecting an old Indian fighter for commander-in-chief. Well, I must stay and see what he does in New York, and I must talk with General Schuyler, and then I must go back to Philadelphia."

Guert was not a statesman, and knew very little about the Continental Congress or Philadelphia; but he did know that General Schuyler was expected to command the patriots of New York.

"I suppose he is my general," he said to Maud that evening; "but General Washington's the man I want to see. He's above Schuyler."

"He is above all our New England generals," said Maud. "I don't see why they put him over General Putnam and General Ward, and all the rest. They are just as good as he is."

"I'm going to see him, somehow," said Guert. "I'll get a chance."

"So will I," replied Maud, but neither of them guessed how Guert's opportunity would come to him.

He had hardly any, when General Washington came ashore from the Jersey ferry-boat next day, for with him came a brilliant escort of military officers and important people, and all the street was lined by militia, presenting arms, and behind these was so dense a crowd that a boy like Guert had no chance at all.

He was disgusted with the very small glimpse he succeeded in getting, and he walked all the way down to the Albany pier to look at what some would have called the other side of the situation. There they were. One large British man-of-war and two smaller ones. They were splendid ships, with rows of port-holes through which cannon looked out threateningly.

"They could knock the city all to pieces," said Guert to himself. "Governor Tryon's on one of them. They say he is coming ashore this evening. Wonder if General Washington will take him prisoner and lock him up."

Jane De Lancey and Rachel Tarns had not for some time been upon speaking terms, but when their carriages met that afternoon, in Bowery Lane, both teams pulled up as if with one accord.

"Rachel," said Miss De Lancey, "your Mr. Washington won't dare to arrest Governor Tryon?"

"Thee may be contented, Jane," said Rachel. "George does not want thy governor. I can tell thee a thing. Our George is a wiser man than thy George."

"Mr. Washington is a traitor," exclaimed Miss De Lancey. "He is a rebel in arms against his king."

"I think thee is wrong, Jane," said Rachel calmly. "I spoke with him, this day" —

"You did?" said Miss De Lancey. "What did he say?"

"He said he believed God would help him do his duty" —

"He had better do his duty to his king," interposed Miss De Lancey.

"He will serve his country," went on Rachel more loudly, but the De Lancey carriage was driving rapidly away.

Guert had failed to get a good look at his commander-in-chief, but he himself had been hunted for and found, and now he was listening to something that made him tingle.

"Go with you and see General Washington?" he asked, as if he was not sure he had heard rightly. "To-night? Why, you don't want me. I can't do a thing."

"Ugh!" said Up-na-tan. "No talk. Come when all heap dark. Keep mouth shut tight, all while."

Guert promised, of course, but he felt, after that, as if he were having some kind of fever. Even his mother declared that it made her nervous when he told her, and she said that he must go, but she did not believe General Washington would see them. It was all fever until an hour or so after dark, and then a kind of chill came to Guert.

That was when he and Up-na-tan and Co-co were met, in the private entry-way of Fraunces' great tavern, down at the corner of Broad and Dock Streets, by Mr. Livingston himself, and were bidden to follow him upstairs. The one question in Guert's mind had been:

"What on earth does Up-na-tan want me here for?"

There was no way of guessing at what might be the

motive of the strange old pirate for almost anything he did, but now Mr. Livingston led the way, and they followed him in silence. Guert felt that his heart was beating very much as it did once before, when he looked over the bulwark of the pirate schooner; but he marched on bravely into the room where he was to see the great general. It was a chamber, behind the great parlor of the tavern. That was crowded with the leading citizens of the province of New York, but there was only one man in this room. He stood by a table, and on the table Guert saw a sword, a pair of epaulets and some writing materials. He saw everything in the room, but he was looking straight at the man, and he was thinking :

"What a man he is!"

He was tall, stern, dignified, with an exceedingly noble face and with eyes that seemed to read even such very hard reading as were Up-na-tan and Co-co. He was dressed in a handsome blue uniform, and he seemed to Guert a very large, powerful man.

Up-na-tan walked straight up to him, without bowing, and when he held out his hand to meet that of Washington the old Manhattan looked as proud and self-possessed as did the general.

The commander-in-chief knew all about Indians. He shook Up-na-tan's hand very gravely, and then turned and shook hands with Co-co and Guert.

Guert was trying to think whether he ought to say

General or Your Excellency, and so did not use any title at all, but stammered out:

"Mother told me to say God bless you, sir, for her."

"Thank your mother, for me, my boy," said Washington kindly, but just then a strange, unearthly sound made Guert twist his head and look at Co-co.

Every shark-tooth in the mouth of the white-wooled Ashantee seemed to be visible, so widely was he grinning, and he was evidently keeping down, with difficulty, a terrible, fierce laugh, such as he might have laughed if he were going into battle. Guert had never seen him look more ferocious, but the general did not mind him at all. He was closely watching the very remarkable movements of Up-na-tan.

The Manhattan had brought with him what appeared to be a pretty heavy parcel, covered with a piece of old calico, and now he opened it, taking out several things which Washington looked at with sudden and strong interest.

"They are Indian scalps," shuddered Guert.

Up-na-tan laid one of them down on the table and said, with fierce emphasis:

"Mohawk!"

Washington nodded, and a look of pain and anxiety shot across his face.

Another of the awful trophies of savage warfare was laid beside the first, and then another and another.

"GOD BLESS THE MOTHERS OF ALL THE BRAVE BOYS OF AMERICA."

"Onondaga!" said Up-na-tan. "Seneca! Oneida! Cayuga! Tuscarora! Huron!"

"All the tribes are against us?" muttered Washington. "This is terrible news."

"Johnson own 'em," said Up-na-tan. "Brandt own 'em. All fight. Kill a heap. Up-na-tan sit down by all Six Nation council-fire. Know 'em all. See 'em all. Want 'em all kill. Say old Manhattan chief no own he island."

"What's that?" inquired Washington.

"Yo, yo!" chuckled Co–co. "So he t'ink. He nebber sell Manhattan. Own dis whole island. Say King George t'ief. Say he stole Up-na-tan land. Want to kill ebbery redcoat."

"Six Nation try to kill Up-na-tan," continued the red man. "Now he help great Colony chief."

There had been something heavy in the calico parcel, and now, as it was lifted forward and put down on the table, it gave a chink that startled Guert, but nothing could startle Washington; not even the opening of that bag and the sight of the English guineas it contained.

"Kidd money," said the Indian. "Great chief take and buy big gun. Buy powder. Kill a heap. What great chief say?"

"Good!" replied Washington calmly. "We will buy guns and powder with it. Tell more about the Iroquois, but not now. Tell General Schuyler. He is to command in New York."

"So, so! Up-na-tan!" replied the Indian. "Tell him heap."

Up to that moment Mr. Livingston had silently stood near the doorway, but now he said:

"Your Excellency, promise him to buy guns with all the money he can bring. There is no doubt of his having been with Kidd. He could arm a ship. Guert and his mother are the only white people he will trust."

"No more, now," said the Indian, as he turned toward the door. "See great chief again, some day. So, so! Up-na-tan!"

"I shall leave him with you and his young friend," said Washington. "But it is a strange way to be supplied with the one thing I needed most, at this hour. At least a thousand guineas for a secret-service fund. We could buy guns in France, if we had anybody to send."

It cost Guert an awful effort to speak, but a thought came that forced him to exclaim, eagerly:

"Your Excellency, if Up-na-tan found the money, Skipper Avery, of New London, would be glad to go. He wants cannon to arm the *Noank*. If he goes to France, may I go with him?"

"I will leave that with General Schuyler and your mother," said Washington, smiling very benevolently at Guert, and he added:

"Chief, good-night."

Up-na-tan again turned and gave a parting handshake with great dignity, while the Ashantee chuckled fiendishly :

"Yo, yo! Up-na-tan dig up heap."

"Good-night, Co-co," said the general, and then he shook hands with Guert.

"Good-night, my boy," he said. "Give my respects to your mother. God bless her, and all the mothers and all the brave boys of America."

Guert could not say a word, but he walked out of the tavern, homeward, feeling as if he had been in a great dream.

CHAPTER VIII.

GUNS AND MEN.

GUERT'S head was almost uncomfortably full of Captain Kidd, French cannon and Yankee privateers. It was hard not to speak a word about them, but Mrs. Ten Eyck herself told him that a soldier ought not to tell war secrets, even to his mother. He could talk with her or with Maud, however, about the Iroquois, and the mischief they might do all along the frontier, and he could say anything he pleased about Washington's looks.

"I'm glad he wore a blue uniform," said Maud, "without a bit of red in it."

Guert's league with Up-na-tan and Co-co seemed to be growing closer, and he had a queer feeling that it made him several years older to talk with them, especially about Skipper Avery and the *Noank*. So many British ships of war were needed for duty at Boston and away down South, that it was safe for almost any craft to visit New York. No more "press-gang" work was now to be feared on shore, although there were continual reports of the stoppage of American vessels at sea, to have their best men taken out "for the king's service."

"She'll get here, one of these days," said Guert to himself. "I wonder what'll happen then? Up-na-tan's waiting for her."

He did not have long to wait; but one of the longest hours Guert had ever known came to him, one day, when he and his friends sat on the Albany pier and watched the *Noank* tacking back and forth in a very light wind, trying to reach her wharf.

"Glad the *Asia's* around in the North River," was the thought in Guert's mind; "but she might send a boat and trap the skipper. They want him."

No British boat came, and the *Noank* was boarded by three pirates who were not in uniform, the moment she touched the wharf. They only had to give a small hint of their errand before the skipper took them down into the cabin, and an excited man was he.

"You needn't say anything ye don't want to," he said, after Guert very carefully opened his business, with Co-co and Up-na-tan watching. "I guess I know something, myself. Everybody knows about them and about Kidd, too. That is, they know and they don't know. Ye couldn't find no better use for that there plunder. I'm ready. I've sailed to France ag'in and ag'in. Jest let me git out this cargo."

He did not actually dance around the cabin, though he looked as if he wanted to do something of the kind; but Guert was feeling very responsible and sober.

"Skipper," he said seriously, "tell you what, you've got to look out. The man-of-war boats patrol all night, they say, and the *Noank* might be visited"—

"Ye-es," drawled the skipper savagely; "she might; you didn't see how many prime men I fetched along. They'd like to 'press this crew. But if they do visit the *Noank* they'll think Lexington and Bunker Hill have got afloat, they will."

Guert had noticed, even in his haste, that the schooner had a great many more men than she needed, but he had hardly thought of them as all "crew."

"They're just what you want, though," he said, "if you're going to France. Are you sure you can get any cannon there?"

"Guns?" exclaimed the skipper. "Why, I tell you what, them there French'd sell their last gun to anybody that would shoot at England with it. Sell it cheap, too. Only they wouldn't want the British to know they'd sold it to us, just now."

Up-na-tan and Co-co did their part of the talking mainly by agreeing to what Guert and the skipper said; but they were evidently in pretty good spirits.

The rest of that day was very long, and so were the following night and all of the next day. Mrs. Ten Eyck again helped Guert explain that he did not intend to come home early, by telling him she did not care how late he staid out if he could help Skipper Avery do anything. After that he felt better and better until a little after dark. Then a queer feeling came over him, for he and Up-na-tan and Co-co were in a stout little cat-boat, sailing away from the side of the *Noank*, and she was anchored well out from the shore of Kip's Bay in the East River. It was dark, for the moon had not yet risen, and there was breeze enough to send such a boat along rapidly.

"We're going," thought Guert. "We're really going to do it."

So they were; but it was a pokerish kind of errand to go on, and it was not long before it became suddenly more so.

Guert saw Up-na-tan take out a large bandana handkerchief and fold it with care.

"Guert cover eyes," he said. "No see Kidd place till he get there. Ugh!"

Guert's heart beat a little quickly, but he had expected to be blindfolded, and he sat still. Then all was utter darkness, and he could hear nothing but the wash of the waves, and now and then a rattle made as the boat tacked this way or that. He could do nothing but wait and think, and it seemed to him that he remembered more pirate stories than he could have believed he knew.

All the tales of the buccaneers and their doings,

and Captain Kidd's cruises, and how much treasure they all captured, and how and where they spent it or hid it, ran through his thoughts until at last he exclaimed, "Oh!" for the boat ran aground.

"Yo, yo!" laughed Co-co. "Heah we are. Heah's de place. All right."

"Guert see plenty, now," said Up-na-tan. "Look a heap."

Off came the handkerchief, and Guert strained his eyes around him in all directions, but there was almost nothing to be seen. Nothing but rocks and a sandy beach with a high bluff beyond.

"It's a kind of long, narrow cove," he said to himself. "I can't guess what shore it's on. Perhaps it's Long Island, but it may be somewhere else. Best kind of hiding-place."

There was no doubt of that, and he knew there were many such places along all the shores of the East River and the Sound. Co-co and Up-na-tan had lighted lanterns, and they stepped ashore, and Guert followed them, carrying a shovel and a hoe. There were pickaxes and crowbars and other tools, but the most important seemed to be a long, strong spar.

"Yo, yo!" chuckled Co-co. "Dah's de ole rock. Turn him ober."

It was so large a rock and so well settled that it could not have been turned over without that long wooden lever.

UP-NA-TAN HANDED OUT BAG AFTER BAG TO CO-CO.

Up-na-tan and Co-co plied their spades and crowbars till they could put one end of the lever well under. After that it seemed to be easy enough; but then, they were both strong men.

Over went the rock, and again the spades were plied, but it was only a few minutes before a large seaman's chest was uncovered. Guert was wild with curiosity; and he thought of all the men who had explored the coast in search of the pirate's treasure.

"But then," he said to himself, "they didn't know where to dig, and there are thousands of rocks like that."

That had been the difficulty. Kidd and his men had a great deal of plunder and they hid it, but beyond that fact the other diggers had known nothing at all. Co-co and Up-na-tan did not say a word as to how they knew, but off came the cover of the chest, and Up-na-tan handed out bag after bag to Co-co and Guert to carry to the boat. Some were as heavy as Guert could carry, but Co-co carried one in each hand, every trip.

"Too much heap silber," growled Up-na-tan. "Gold buy more gun. Skipper get all he can. Hope he steal some."

Guert himself wished for gold instead of silver, and was glad to know that some of the bags were more precious than others, but then they were smaller bags.

"I don't know what the price of cannon is," he

thought, " but I guess the skipper can arm the *Noank* and more, too. Don't I wish I could go with him! I will, too, some day, after the *Noank* is turned into a cruiser."

It did not seem exactly real, however, even when he saw the chest shut up, the sand shoveled back, and the great rock tipped back into its place.

" There," he exclaimed, " I see, now. The tide's coming in. We got here at low water. At high tide that rock'll be almost covered under."

That was the very simple secret of the security of the pirate's hiding-place, and the cover of the chest had been water-tight.

" Oh! " exclaimed Guert again, but the bandana was put over his eyes the moment he entered the boat, and he knew no more about the exact place of that cove than he did before.

" There's a big, three-cornered rock at the foot of the bluff," he said to himself. " It's just at high-water mark. I guess I'd know that rock. I could hunt for it, some day."

The motion of the boat told him that the wind was still good, but again it seemed as if they were making a dreadfully long trip, and his friends were as silent as if they were a pair of mummies.

" Look! " exclaimed Up-na-tan, at last; and Guert jerked off his bandage.

" Why, there's the *Noank*, isn't it? " asked Guert.

"The moon has risen, too. What are we to do next?"

"Ugh!" replied Up-na-tan. "See skipper."

That was more than Guert could do; but one of the cabin portholes was open, and the boat was quickly rocking under that small window, while Up-na-tan passed through it all the bags in swift succession. It was marvelous how rapidly the precious but dangerous cargo of the sail-boat went into the cabin of the *Noank*.

Before that task was half done, Guert was on board, talking with the old "harpooneer" mate.

"We're all ready to get off," said the mate, "but I jist dew wish one o' them there press-gang patrol-boats'd try their tricks on us, this trip."

"What for?" asked Guert.

"Why," said the mate, "we're so all-killin' ready for 'em. Hurrah! If that isn't one on 'em, I'm mistaken. Boys, all of ye git down below. Boat comin'!"

Just then Up-na-tan and Co-co sprang upon the deck, with precisely a similar warning, and a moment more Skipper Avery came up from his cabin in a fiery excitement.

"Guert," he said, "take that musket. Now you see if we don't show 'em something. We'll teach 'em how to 'press Yankees."

Swiftly over the water, in the brightening moonlight,

came one of the well-manned boats of a British man-of-war, and the first words uttered by the officer in command proved that it was more than a mere press-gang, for he said:

"Right aboard, men. We'll search her first and 'tend to the 'pressing afterwards."

"Reckon so," growled Skipper Avery. "You can s'arch her. It's wuth your while."

He had hardly needed to give an order to his men, for there seemed to be a good understanding among them, and only two or three were to be seen when the British boat came alongside and its crew clambered to the deck of the *Noank*.

"Got ye this time, you old rebel," shouted the British lieutenant. "You didn't know the old *Merlin* was in the harbor, did ye?"

"What are ye goin' to do?" asked Skipper Avery calmly. "You've no right to take this craft, nor anything aboard of her."

"Bo's'n," roared the lieutenant, "you and your squad hold the deck. I'll go below" —

Down he went, without answering the skipper, and he was followed by six stalwart seamen, with drawn cutlasses, leaving but four on deck.

"Bunker Hill!" shouted Skipper Avery.

Up flew a sail that lay on the shadowy deck, forward, and it seemed as if all the rest of the *Noank's* upper works had been a kind of coop, for men came out of them, almost anywhere. There had been six under the sail, and the British boatswain and his four men found themselves looking by the light of several lanterns into the muzzles of more than a dozen muskets.

"Drop your cutlasses, boys," said the skipper. "We won't hurt ye, but if you lift a hand you are dead men."

"No use, boys," said the boatswain. "We're done for. It's a trap."

"Bunker Hill!" shouted Skipper Avery down the companionway, and up sprang the astonished lieutenant, only to almost run his nose against the muzzle of Guert's musket, and to see the long knife of Up-na-tan gleaming within a hand-breadth of his throat.

"Surrender!" yelled the skipper.

"I surrender!" gasped the lieutenant.

It was well he did, for Co-co was making a plunge motion at him with a wicked-looking whaling-lance. It was all over without firing a shot. Even two seamen who had been left in the ship's boat were ordered on board. Every weapon, the lanterns, and all the boat oars except one pair, were kept as war plunder.

"Now, boys," said Skipper Avery, "I don't want to 'press any British sailor, but if any of ye are 'pressed Yankees, now's yer time. I don't want the lieutenant, anyhow. King George can keep him."

"He won't keep me," shouted one of the sailors,

stepping in among the crew of the *Noank*. "I'm from Marble'ead."

"I'm from Salem;" and another said "Nantucket," and another "Baltimore."

"Bully!" exclaimed Guert; but just then the boatswain himself stepped out.

"Don't ye know me, Lyme Avery?" he asked. "Do ye s'pose I'd stay an hour among 'em, if I could git away?"

"Vinc Prentice!" shouted the skipper. "Hev I got you out o' their clutches? Won't old Sam and yer mother be glad? You'll sail with me, you will?"

"You'll all sail with ropes around your necks," growled the lieutenant. "Don't you dare keep those men" —

"Keep tongue still in mouth," came from Up-na-tan, just then, in a fierce, low tone. "Heap fool! No talk. Get into boat 'fore have head cut off" — and as if he could not restrain it any longer, out sprang the war-whoop of the Manhattans.

"Get along, Lieutenant," said Skipper Avery. "You won't need any rope if you cross the paths of some men I know. I can keep his hand from you now, if you go peaceably; don't ye wait, though."

Down into their own boat went the officer and little more than half the men he had brought with him, but the anchor of the *Noank* was already up and her crew were hoisting the mainsail.

"We shall look in at New London," said the skipper, as Guert and his friends got down into their cat-boat. "Then hurrah for France and the guns! Good-by!"

"Whoop!" yelled the Manhattan. "Buy heap big gun! Kill a heap! So, so, Up-na-tan"—and another ringing war-whoop and the Ashantee battle-cry drowned Guert's shout of farewell, while the schooner swung away in one direction, and the dismal looking boat-load of disarmed British tars tugged against the tide toward the distant *Merlin* with their one pair of oars.

It was in the gray of the dawn that Guert reached home, and even after his mother came downstairs it seemed to him as if a kind of mist were floating around him. He could not make it real that he had been seeing and doing the things that he remembered since yesterday. He did not mean to tell too much of it, and he hardly knew how much he had told until at last Mrs. Ten Eyck said:

"Guert! I was thinking—pirates! What dreadful things they must have done before all that gold and silver got there! I'm glad it's going to be used in a good cause, anyhow."

"'Tis, if the skipper can get the guns," said Guert, "and he says he can."

"But, Guert," remarked his mother, "you didn't know about Maud. Her folks sent for her and she's gone home to Connecticut. She won't be back till next winter."

Guert was out and out sorry for that. He had been studying desperately just how much he could tell Maud about his night's wonderful work, and now he could not tell her anything. If, however, he was disappointed that morning, she was not. She was in the best of spirits and very busy, for she was the center of a room full of neighbors and relations who were making her tell them all the news from New York.

She seemed to know it all pretty well, up to the hour she left. It was a pity, too, that she could not have put in the last doings of her boy neighbor, for she spoke of him again and again, remarking of him:

"He goes everywhere, and a girl can't, and he knows everything that's going on. I wish he were here. He could tell you all about it" — and she was manifestly proud of a boy who had actually boarded a tea ship and a provision ship, had helped steal barrels of British powder, had ridden Paul Revere's horse with dispatches, and who owned a gun that had kicked her over. What would they have thought of him if they could have known the very things that she knew no more about than they did?

It was a little curious that it did not seem to Guert as if it amounted to anything. Maud told her friends:

"He's a splendid fellow, and he's tall for his age. So strong, too; and he isn't afraid of anything."

He himself remarked to Rachel Tarns :

"I ain't worth much more'n a button, anyhow. Even Aleck Hamilton won't take me into his company. Says I've got to wait till I'm older."

Rachel looked at him almost sadly, for a moment, before she said :

"Thee is in too much haste, Guert. Thee grows fast. Let me tell thee a thing. Men get killed in war. I like thy friend Nathan Hale. He gave thee good advice about thy books. He is a good teacher. Get thee ready to take his place. Some day it may be given him to pay his life as a ransom for the liberty of his country. The war before us is long, and thee will be a man before it is over."

Tall and dark and grim was the patriotic Quakeress, but it struck Guert then that she was handsome, as she spoke, with the flush on her cheeks and the fire in her eyes. She was as handsome as Nathan Hale.

He could not quite take her advice amid all the excitement. It was not easy to be in the house a great deal of the time, or to study books instead of soldiers and war.

One of his friends was studying military affairs, and there was something very curious about the ways and doings of Up-na-tan. He could not have been any more reserved than formerly, but he certainly had become more haughty. He did not exactly put on war-paint, but he no longer wore a red calico shirt, and the blue one he substituted was fairly new, and clean most of the time. His leggings, too, were better fringed, and the new straw hat he obtained had a blue ribbon and a stamped silver ornament. He refused to do any more farm work, although he would sometimes go fishing. His especial delight seemed to be the inspection of any military works that were being made for the defense of Manhattan Island. They were his, and all the men in them were there to defend his property. He seemed, moreover, to have almost a personal affection for a cannon. At least, Guert had never seen him pat or caress anything else, but when he said so he was answered :

" Heap gun, kill a heap. Skipper buy some in France. Bring back cannon cargo. Old chief know gun. Long gun on Kidd ship. Heap shoot."

The largest cannon were at the Battery, twenty-one of them ; and when, late in August, they were all removed to a safer place, in the new works on the heights, in the upper part of the island, Up-na-tan and Co-co went with them, all the way. Before they returned, Guert had heard the news. There had been a fight with a barge-load of men from the British man-of-war *Asia.* There had been cannonading from the ship, and men had been killed and wounded on both sides, but both were disposed to lay the blame on each other for firing first.

" Guert boy," said the Indian, when he was asked

about it, at the Ten Eyck place, "Up-na-tan great chief. Shoot redcoat. No let 'em get big gun. Kill one, anyhow. So, so, Up-na-tan!"

Only a few weeks later, Governor Tryon himself gave up pretending to live in New York. He left his house, on Broad Street, and took up his residence upon one of the ships; but those were now almost cut off from all shore supplies. Even the most sincere Royalists no longer dared to sell milk and vegetables to the soldiers and sailors of their king. There were constant rumors that the fleet intended to bombard the town, and several times, when a salute was fired, women and children in the lower wards ran out crying into the streets, believing that the work of destruction had begun.

More and more of the people moved away, especially the richer people, until it was said that a third of all were gone; and the winter came very cold, very dull and very gloomy, to New York. Gloomy and cold and hard was that first winter of the great war. Even such news as came from the half-starved army in the American camps around Boston made things seem gloomier.

Guert had a pretty good reason for being often at Mrs. Murray's during the second week in January, and one afternoon he had just remarked:

"Mother spins and weaves till she doesn't seem to want to go to bed at all."

"I don't know how to weave, or I would," sighed Mrs. Murray. "But how I do wish Maud would come. They wrote that she might be here any day, now the sleighing is so good."

"Hark!" exclaimed Guert. "Sleigh bells?"

"Guert!" shouted Mrs. Murray, after a quick glance through a window, "there she comes. Maud is here."

He was already springing toward the door, and she heard him say:

"Ain't I glad? And she'll bring all the news from New England."

Of course she would, and she was out of the sleigh and up the piazza steps like a flash, but the first news she told, after Mrs. Murray gave her a chance to tell anything, belonged to New York.

"Aunt Murray!" she said, "Guert! what do you think? I met Stephen De Lancey and his Aunt Jane driving up the Bloomingdale Road in their sleigh. He said Mr. Lee and his rebels are marching in, down town, and he wouldn't stay there to see them" —

"General Lee?" shouted Guert. "Our army has come! There'll be better times now."

"Of course there will," said Maud; "but, Guert, Aaron Burr's with General Montgomery, in Canada. He has distinguished himself. They captured Montreal, and they took prisoners" —

"Wish I'd been there," groaned Guert.

"You'd wish you were not, then," said Mrs. Murray, "fighting in such weather as this is; Canada weather, too! Now, Maud, do tell us everything."

"And then you must come over and see mother," said Guert, "and tell her" —

"Of course I will," said Maud; but even the Boston news could not detain him long, for he was all in a fever to see what he called "the American army."

He saw it all before night, for there were only about twelve hundred men. They were pretty warmly clad, but not in anything like uniform. What they needed most was guns with bayonets, and cannon for any forts they might build. So Guert told his mother, that evening, just before she went over to Mrs. Murray's for another news-talk.

"We are all going down for a look at them to-morrow," she said. "Maud, and Rachel Tarns, and all of us."

"You'll ride," said Guert. "I'll be down there, somewhere."

He meant to be, but he had no idea of just where they were to find him, or in what company. It seemed to him that he dreamed all night about the winter fights at Boston and in Canada, and he woke up wondering if there were to be any in New York, now the troops had come.

"I'll see them parade on the Common, anyhow," he said.

He set out early; but hardly had he left his own gate before a voice behind him hailed him gruffly with:

"So! go 'long! Old chief show Guert when he get there."

"Show me what?" asked Guert; but there was no answer to that question.

Sleighloads of all kinds of people went by them, for almost everybody was willing to look at that parade, and when they reached the Bowery Lane side of the Common they found it already lined with sightseers.

"Come," said Up-na-tan; and Guert followed him across the street, to where quite a group of officers and citizens were gathered. He had not heard a woman's voice in one of the sleighs saying, "Let's go over and see what it is."

"Look!" said Up-na-tan. "Big gun. No come across water. Colony men make. Heap fire. Heap old bell. Up-na-tan watch 'em long time."

Guert did indeed look, with sudden interest, for there, laid out in a glittering row upon the snow and ice, were more than a dozen new brass cannon.

"Splendid achievement of our first American foundry!" exclaimed one of the gentlemen. "We are making saltpeter, too, and we can furnish our own gunpowder. The liberties of America are safe, if we can mold our own cannon."

Forward stepped the Manhattan, and deliberately paced the length of one of the brilliant weapons of war.

"Ugh!" he said. "Heap short. Melt one bell. Want more bell. Want heap big gun for fort. Long gun for ship. Where find bell?"

"That's so!" exclaimed an officer. "He has hit it. We're short of brass. They're nothing but field guns."

The deep gloom on Up-na-tan's face may have had jealousy in it, for he brightened exceedingly as he said:

"Long gun come. Buy 'em across big water. French. Heap shoot. So, so, Up-na-tan!"

"He has hit it again," said the officer, as the Manhattan strode proudly away.

"Guert," said Rachel, when he walked up to her sleigh, "I'm glad thee saw those guns. It is against the law for thy people to mold in brass or in iron. Thee may not make anything for thyself. Thee must buy it of thy king's people that live on his island. Thee had to learn to cast cannon before he would let thee make kettles."

Guert was not listening very well.

"What we want is brass," he muttered, as she ended. "I must speak to Maud."

She was beckoning him, eagerly, from the Murray sleigh, and the brass and cannon question had to wait.

"Guert," she said, "you know poor Mr. Avery, the skipper. I've just heard of him, from a New London man. He went on a voyage to France, in his schooner, and on his way back a British cruiser captured him. They haven't heard of him since."

"Captured?" groaned Guert. "I'm so sorry. That's awful."

"Isn't it?" she said. "What if they should impress him and all his men?"

"Did they get them all?" he asked.

"Nobody knows," replied Maud; "but they took the *Noank*, and she's in Boston Harbor now."

Guert turned away as if he did not care to hear any more; but he was thinking:

"They will hang him. What shall I say to Up-na-tan?"

CHAPTER IX.

THE SCOUTING PARTY.

THE more Guert thought about the bad tidings concerning Skipper Avery and the *Noank*, the less he felt like telling them to Up-na-tan and Co-co.

"There are such lots of things that may have happened," he said to himself. "Maybe they didn't buy any guns. Maybe they bought some and didn't have them on board. Perhaps they sent them here on another ship."

At all events, he knew that a great deal of news came which turned out untrue, and he could afford to wait until there was some kind of certainty. Still, he he had a dream one night of seeing the *Noank* armed with more and bigger brass cannon than a craft of her size would think of carrying except as heavy freight.

The next tidings from the American army in Canada was very sad, for it told of General Montgomery's defeat and death at Quebec. There was, at first, no certainty as to who else had been killed, and Guert and Maud and all the rest were left in doubt as to whether they were ever again to see their friends.

It was doubt, doubt, about all manner of things, until one fine spring morning, when Rachel Tarns came hurrying through the gate of the Ten Eyck place, followed closely by Mrs. Murray and Maud.

"Mother!" shouted Guert, as he darted out to meet them. "Come out here, right away! Something's happened!"

"News?" she exclaimed, and the spinning-wheel was left to whirl itself to a rest, while the cat chased a ball of yarn away into the kitchen.

"Anneke," asked Rachel, "how is thee?"

"I'm well enough," replied Mrs. Ten Eyck. "Tell me what it is."

"Aaron wasn't killed," said Maud.

"The British have been driven out of Boston," said Mrs. Murray.

"Alexander has been commissioned captain of one of the New York artillery companies," said Rachel proudly. "But Aaron did not lose the gray mare. He did not take her with him to Canada at all. He had to run away on foot."

"Guert," said Maud, "and they say all the British fleet and army are coming to New York, and that all our army, and General Washington, are coming to keep them from capturing us. There's going to be more fighting here than ever there was at Boston."

"Hurrah for Aleck Hamilton!" shouted Guert. "I was sure he'd get it. His men are all ready, too. It's real good about Aaron" — and then there was a general jumble of all that was known, as yet, concerning the triumph at Boston and all the other movements of armies, at the south as well as at the north.

Boy as he was, Alexander had indeed been given his commission, but only after a sharp examination by officers of experience, who discovered what good use he had made of the military books bought for him by Rachel Tarns. Perhaps one point in his favor was that his company was already in very good condition for him to command.

Great was the pride of Rachel, but Guert's first exultation changed shortly into almost a moody state of mind, for regiment after regiment came marching into New York, and he did not belong to any of them.

It was a tremendous army, it seemed to him, and it was growing larger every day, and there was no end to the forts and batteries that were building. Even over on the high ground, across the East River, beyond the village of Brooklyn, there was already a line of strong earthworks, and Guert went over to see them more than once.

"If the redcoats ever come here," he thought, "we shall beat them all to pieces."

His own satisfaction, however, was as nothing to Up-na-tan's approval of the manner in which the "colony men" were preparing to defend his island. He seemed to own it more than ever, although he sharply criticised all the works because of their lack of "heap long gun."

More and more of the people moved out as the soldiers marched in, and all the ordinary society affairs of the city were entirely broken up. Commerce did not altogether cease, for ships could come and go by way of Long Island Sound. Out in that direction, indeed, there was a fleet of American cruisers forming, that was not at all like the British fleet in the Lower Bay, but that promised to be of good service. It consisted of coasting schooners, sloops, row-galleys and whale boats, manned by daring fellows who were ready to capture anything smaller than a man-of-war, or even that, if they could catch it napping. Whenever Guert got a good look into one of those craft he thought of the *Noank* and felt badly, and half wished he could be a sailor.

The weeks went by like a dream, and one day was like another, there was so much excitement. Mrs. Ten Eyck herself was hardly surprised when, one April afternoon, the Murray carriage came to her gate, and Rachel marched in to say :

"Anneke, thee must come with us. Israel Putnam came yesterday, to command thy king's troops that are protecting his colonists against their enemies. We are going to visit his wife and daughters, and thee must go with us. Guert, thee may get up and ride with Sarah's driver."

Mrs. Ten Eyck was quickly ready, and all the way down town Guert was busily explaining to Maud, rather than to the older ladies, the distribution of the American forces. They seemed to be camped everywhere.

General Putnam's headquarters were at the old Kennedy mansion, at the very lower end of Broadway, and when the carriage pulled up in front of it, Maud exclaimed:

"Why, the house is full of soldiers. Does Mrs. Putnam really live here?"

There was indeed a garrison look about it, and a strong guard party had just halted at the entrance; but Maud's answer came from Guert, as a tall, fine-looking young officer who commanded them went through the process of changing the headquarter's sentries.

"Nathan Hale!" exclaimed Guert. "There he is, Maud. He's a captain."

"I am here, Guert," laughed the captain, as he turned and lifted his hat to the ladies. He could not have heard Mrs. Murray whisper to Rachel:

"How very handsome he is!" but he added to Guert:

"I'm on duty now. Come and see me as soon as you can at the camp of Knowlton's regiment. I want a talk."

"So do I," shouted Guert. "I've all sorts of things to tell."

"Forward, march!" said Hale to his men at that moment, and he only bowed again to the carriage load, as they moved away.

"He is splendid!" exclaimed Maud, but they were all getting down to go into the house — all excepting Guert, who was not expected to call on Mrs. Putnam.

There were no other lady-callers there at that hour, nor was the general's wife ready for any, apparently. All the front rooms on the lower floor were full of busy army officers, but a soldier very politely invited Mrs. Murray and her friends to follow him.

"Hear that?" said Mrs. Ten Eyck.

"It's the sound of a loom," exclaimed Mrs. Murray. "Somebody is weaving."

"Weaving in a fort?" whispered Maud, but on they went into a large room in the rear.

There were several women in it, older and younger, and the loom ceased as one of them left it to welcome the visitors.

"Thee is Israel Putnam's wife?" said Rachel, with great energy. "Thee is like thy good husband. This is Anneke Ten Eyck, and this is Sarah Murray. Thee knows Maud Wolcott. Thee can talk with them, but thy loom need not waste any time. I can beat thee weaving."

Perhaps she could. At all events she took Mrs.

Putnam's place at the loom, and the business of making linen for soldiers did not cease, nor did that of the Putnam girls at their spinning-wheels.

The talk and the work went on together, with the most patriotic cheerfulness, for Mrs. Putnam was all smiles and good humor, and Rachel did not at all lose her part of the conversation.

Out at the door Guert found something to do that he had not expected.

"Glad to see boy," said somebody behind him suddenly. "Up-na-tan want talk with old man Putnam. Co-co, too."

"I can fix it," exclaimed Guert, and a word to the sentry brought out the officer of the guard.

"Information?" said the officer, in reply to Guert's explanation. "Saw General Washington about it once, did he? Bring him and the black fellow right in."

In a moment more they were all standing before General Putnam, to whom Up-na-tan held out a hand as frankly as if he had known him for years.

The old Indian fighter shook it as frankly, and the Manhattan reported at once.

"Heap spy all over island. Up-na-tan find 'em. Co-co find 'em."

"Can't help it," said the general. "Every Tory is a spy. Can't shut 'em all up."

"Stop some," said Up-na-tan. "Stop boat go to

ship at night. Tell heap. Up-na-tan want good boat. Watch 'em!"

"Colonel," said Putnam sharply, to another officer, "see that these men have a good boat to patrol with. They are the best scouts we could get. The chief may report to me at any time."

Out went the queer squad of scouts, and Guert was suddenly aware that he and his friends had somehow joined the American army and navy, and were to operate against the British fleet.

"It will be one thing more to tell Captain Hale," he thought. "I must go and see him as soon as I can. We can scout all over the bay. Even a boy can steer a boat, and my eyes are as good as Up-na-tan's daytimes; but Co-co and he can see after dark."

Mrs. Murray's party of patriotic women finished their visit with Mrs. Putnam and her daughters, but when they went out there was no Guert to go with them. When he did get back to his own house late that evening, he had a great story to tell of the visit he had made at Captain Hale's quarters, with Co-co and Up-na-tan, and of the very fine, swift-running little boat in which the chief and his crew were to watch for spies from the fleet.

"Captain Hale wants to go with us as often as he can," he said. "Up-na-tan has taken the greatest liking to him. Mother, you will let me go?"

"Of course I will," exclaimed Mrs. Ten Eyck.

"I've been wanting to have you do something. Wouldn't Mrs. Putnam send a boy of hers?"

"She would!" said Guert. "Guess I'm as good an American as any Putnam is. But what on earth do they all mean by saying that we are still under King George, when we are fighting him?"

That was a question that was greatly troubling older heads than his. All the British, and a great many Americans, still insisted that Mr. Washington could not be a "general" without a commission from the king. He was only the leader of an armed mob of rebel colonists, and he and all of them ought to be hung for treason.

That was one of the words that Maud Wolcott was trying to understand, and Rachel Tarns helped her when she said:

"If thee can hear thyself talk, thee ought to know. Thee talks treason all the while. Thee is as bad a rebel as George Washington."

Mrs. Ten Eyck did not see very much of her son during some weeks after that. He was away from home at night very often, and he would not always tell even Maud where he had been. He did succeed, however, in making her say of him, to Mrs. Murray:

"How Guert is growing. He won't be a boy much longer. I'm glad Captain Hale goes with them so much."

It was only now and then that he could do so, and

there came one especial occasion that he had missed. Only the original crew of the scout-boat were tramping wearily along Broad Street when Guert remarked:

"We won't go to Putnam this time."

"Ugh!" said Up-na-tan. "No. Go see great chief. Heap big talk."

Very gloomy and very haughty seemed the last of the Manhattans, that morning when they reached the headquarters of the Commander-in-Chief. He seemed to be giving orders to the sergeant of the guard, instead of asking for anything.

"Go!" he said. "Tell great chief Up-na-tan!"

The sergeant did go, but in a moment more a short, slight young fellow, in the uniform of a lieutenant-colonel stepped lightly out, exclaiming:

"Guert? You here?"

"Aaron! Colonel Burr!" responded Guert in great astonishment. "We want to see the General."

"I'm on his staff," said Aaron. "I'll ask him, but he hardly sees anybody."

He went and he came again, and now he was all a soldier on duty, and not an acquaintance, in his manner, as he led the way and told them to follow. He must have said something in the way of explanation, however, for once more Guert and his friends were alone in the room with the Commander-in-Chief.

He had a worn, stern look, and his face did not relax in a smile as he slightly nodded to them, saying:

"Up-na-tan, speak."

"Up-na-tan tell," said the red man, as dignifiedly. "Two night ago, Bedloe Island. Up-na-tan, Co-co, Guert. See boat come from ship. See more boat come down river. See Iroquois chief land on Bedloe. See Johnson chief. Not know Guy Johnson. Mebbe other paleface Iroquois. See Tryon land on Bedloe. Not hear talk. Too far. All talk and go away. Up-na-tan follow to Lower Bay. Co-co follow no. Wait on Bedloe in rocks."

He motioned explanations as he spoke, and Washington's face grew dark as he listened.

"Orderly!" he said, loudly, and the door opened and a tall soldier in the uniform of the "bodyguard" stepped in and stood at a salute, awaiting orders.

"Tell Colonel Burr to come here."

"Ugh!" suddenly exclaimed Up-na-tan, glaring at the soldier and pointing at him fiercely. "That man! Up-na-tan see him on Bedloe. See him talk Tryon. Watch him come to shore. Not know him then. Know now."

Down sank the soldier into the nearest chair, like a fainting man; but Burr had heard and was entering the room.

"Colonel Burr," said Washington, "put Hickey in irons. Search him. This is Tryon's plot for a Tory rising, on the arrival of Howe and the fleet. On no account let it be known precisely how it was discovered.

Take him out. We must convict him without the testimony of these men. They must not be suspected."

Up-na-tan nodded, understanding the need for keeping his services a secret, but he spoke again:

"Great chief of Manhattans send to France for gun. Send heap Kidd money. Think lose gun. Not know yet. Send again, some day. Go, now. Do more to-night. Not want talk."

He did not go without hearty thanks to all three of them; but Washington might well be sick at heart when the plots and treachery around him had penetrated and corrupted men of his own trusted bodyguard, chosen for supposed fidelity.

There had not been a great deal for Guert to say, and he was glad of it, for he felt with more than a little oppression what a mere boy he was in the presence of the greatest man in America.

"Oh! but isn't he a great man," he said to his mother, when he told her about Hickey and the discovery of the plot.

"I am so glad," she said, "that you have really been able to do something."

He had no idea what he might be called upon to do next; but only two nights afterwards he was out in the scout-boat, feeling that somebody else was captain of it. When only Up-na-tan and Co-co were with him, he was all the while aware that he was the only white man on board, and that so he outranked them a little, even if he left the direction of things to the old Manhattan.

This night, however, he felt peculiarly conscious of the heroic presence of Nathan Hale, and that there was only one commander of the expedition.

There was not much commanding to do for a while, for the boat crept silently along shore, on the Brooklyn side, keeping in the shadow of it as much as possible, until, at last, it made a quick run out through Buttermilk Channel. After that there was not much more boating to be done, that night.

Just as the sun arose next morning, three men and a boy were lying, very quietly, among some bushes at the bottom of a bluff that looked out upon the Lower Bay of New York. Several ships lay at anchor, here and there, and from each there fluttered gayly out the red cross flag of England, the mistress of the seas, and, as yet, the mistress of all the American colonies.

"They are bully good ships," said Guert.

"So they are," muttered Captain Hale, as he scanned them carefully through the telescope he had brought with him. "We know all about these fellows, but Howe's fleet must be close at hand, now."

"Ugh!" exclaimed Up-na-tan sharply. "Heap more sail."

Guert strained his eyes vainly at the misty distance; but those of the Indian could be trusted, for Hale changed the direction of his glass, and said at once:

"That's so; there they come. The Staten Island lookout must have seen them first, but we must wait and find out all we can."

"I guess there are plenty of Tories, too, all along shore. 'Twouldn't do to be caught."

"We won't be caught," said Hale cheerfully.

"They might hang us for spies," suggested Guert; "just as General Washington had Hickey hung, yesterday."

"No, they wouldn't," replied Hale. "A scout is a scout, and a spy is a spy. I'm in full uniform and we are all armed. We'd be prisoners of war."

"I guess that'd be bad enough," said Guert. "I can see 'em, now. There's going to be a swarm of 'em."

Hour after hour the four scouts lay in their covert, while the splendid British fleet came sweeping into the bay. Hale's telescope was busy, and every now and then he pencilled, in his memorandum book, notes of the kind and number of the ships. There were men-of-war, of several sizes, transport ships, supply ships; and they and others closely following them were bringing a great army to capture Manhattan Island, and to take it away from Mr. Washington and his army, and from the Continental Congress, and from old Up-na-tan.

The breeze was favorable, and the naval commanders took advantage of it to sail right along in search of safe anchorages, not too near each other.

"HOWE'S FLEET MUST BE CLOSE AT HAND."

Hale continued his work of observation, with his telescope and note-book, and Guert stared dreamily at the great fleet, until he was startled by a savagely angry exclamation at his side.

"Ugh! Ugh!" growled Up-na-tan. "Look! *Noank!* Lose all heap gun!"

Captain Hale already knew the story of the New London skipper, and he aimed his glass in the direction pointed out. "It is a fact," he said; "there she comes. What a pity it is about Lyme Avery!"

Anchors had gone down rapidly, and there were now many boats going to and fro among the ships. Quite a number of boats seemed also to propose trips toward the shores of Staten Island and Long Island. Each of these latter was full of soldiers as well as seamen. They were so many scouting parties sent out to find out what might be upon the nearest land; but Guert was hardly noticing them, for he was saying to himself:

"Maybe that's the *Noank*. I can hardly be sure, among so many. It's too bad."

He had hardly cared for one tall and stately war-ship, lying nearer than the rest, but a boat sent out from her had headed straight toward a kind of break in the bluff shore, not far from the covert of the four watchers. Hale's glass was pointed at that boat for several minutes, but he made no remark until after she touched the beach. An officer and some soldiers and seamen stepped out of her and marched up through the gap, leaving her in charge of a midshipman and a brace of sailors. Then Captain Hale put down his glass with a long breath, as he hoarsely whispered:

"Lyme Avery! He is one of the men down there by the boat."

"'Kipper!" said the Manhattan. "Ugh! Look!"

"Yo, yo!" gurgled Co-co. "Dah he is."

"Now's our chance," said Hale. "We must get him away from them. The redcoats are out of sight over the bluff."

He put his fingers to his lips and blew a long, peculiar whistle, but Guert did not know that it was one of the signal calls of the Connecticut "minute men." He felt very much, however, as if somebody had set him on fire and that he was burning very well. The next moment he was creeping along on all-fours behind Nathan Hale, with Co-co and Up-na-tan just ahead.

"They are better bushfighters than we are, Guert," said Hale. "See there?"

Guert saw one of the two men at the boat lay down his musket to tighten his belt. In an instant he saw the other hurl his own musket into the water, snatch up the first man's gun and turn and point it at the disarmed seaman and midshipman. It was also as if a pair of human panthers went bounding across the few yards between the bushes and the boat.

"Don't hurt 'em," Guert heard Skipper Avery

say, as he and Hale darted forward. "Tie 'em up and gag 'em."

"No speak," growled Up-na-tan, and the long, gleaming knife in his hand and another in Co-co's explained his terrible meaning.

Before the boy officer could fairly know what was happening, he was sitting on a rock with his hands tied behind him and a handkerchief over his mouth.

"Yiz nadn't toie me very toight," said the sailor. "Oim from Kerry. "Id go wid yiz ave it wasn't yiz was all to be baten. I'd be ownly took again and they'd hong me for desartin'. Get along wid yiz."

That was just what they did, the four American scouts, taking the skipper with them, after Co-co had knocked a hole in the bottom of the boat with a stone.

"Yo, yo!" he laughed fiercely. "They nebber follar Co-co 'long shoah."

That meant something, for the first race of the fugitives was along the beach for some distance before they struck out into some woods.

Their daring feat was discovered within five minutes, however, and they were then followed by a force strong enough to have made their position perilous if it had not been for so good a start, and for their knowledge of the ground.

"The main thing is to keep out of sight," said Hale. "Their muskets would reach us. Down, Guert! There they are!"

Down they went, in a dense thicket of sumach bushes, and it seemed to Guert that he hardly breathed while a British officer and half a dozen soldiers, with four seamen, marched rapidly past them, within a stone's throw. He and his friends were well armed, but they would have been hopelessly outnumbered.

"Ugh!" muttered Up-na-tan. "Old Van Brunt barn. Lobster think we go there. Come!"

He seemed to glide away through the bushes and underbrush, and the others imitated him as well as they could, while their pursuers wasted time in a somewhat cautious inspection of the old barn.

"We are all right now," said Skipper Avery at last. "I'm glad Co-co didn't knife that poor middy. He is the son of an earl, and he may be an admiral some day. I've had an awful time."

It was almost the first thing he had said, for he had been evidently under strong excitement. He was looking in pretty good health, but there was an expression in his frank, honest face, which Guert had never seen there before.

"Did they say you were a deserter?" asked Hale.

"No; they didn't," said the skipper, "for I'd never been on any ship's list. I'd only got away from a press-gang. But they'd have hung the other boys. Vine Prentice and four of 'em took the cutter and went. I hope they got into Havre all right, but I don't know. They're hard on deserters, just now, and the way they treat 'pressed Yankees! Well, I won't say any more about it. They'd no lawful right to seize the *Noank*, anyhow. They just took her, law or no law."

"Where heap gun?" inquired Up-na-tan, with almost mournful earnestness. "Gone?"

The skipper turned and pointed toward the Lower Bay and said:

"They turned me into the *Saragossa* and they made a supply boat of the *Noank*. There she is, out there, packed with provisions for their army. We bought the guns, but the French wouldn't let us mount any of 'em in a French harbor. So we stowed them down in the hold, under the ballast. There they are now, with a cargo of salt beef and flour on top of 'em."

"Ugh!" said Up-na-tan. "Good. Know where gun. Get *Noank*, some day."

"I believe we must try and do that very thing," exclaimed Hale.

"Guess we will," said Guert. "What our army wants most is guns."

"What I want most is the *Noank* with guns on her," growled Skipper Avery. "If I can make a privateer of her, I'll teach 'em what it means to keep a New London whaler in irons a month, and then flog him for calling himself a free man. That isn't the worst of it. I don't want our New London folks to know what's become of some of our boys."

"I don't want to know," said Hale sadly. "This war is getting more bitter every day. We shall be as savage as Up-na-tan before it's over, I'm afraid."

They were going right along, as they talked, and their peril was about over, for their pursuers had found the barn empty, and were holding a council of war as to which way they had better march next.

"Yer honor," remarked the Kerryman to the officer, "wan of 'em's a red skin, an' ye'll not find 'em. They've tuk to the wuds. You'd all be skelped."

"The woods may be full of Indians, for all we know," said the officer thoughtfully. "I've no right to lead my men into an ambuscade. I mustn't forget how they murdered us at Lexington. Back to the boat, men! March!"

He was only prudent in remembering the bad things which had happened to British soldiers among woods and thickets and stone farm walls; but the party he was following had not planned any ambuscade. They were now only working their way along the shore to the swampy little inlet where their own boat lay. It was no longer unsafe to talk, and there were many things to be said.

Every now and then some exclamation from Up-na-tan and a fierce glitter in his eyes was followed by references to the *Noank* and to the treasure of cannon in her hold, and Co-co laughed back, as exultingly as if there were no doubt whatever of recapturing them.

They were running through the Buttermilk Channel, homeward, when Hale remarked to the skipper:

"Lyme Avery, General Howe has brought too many men. I'm afraid Washington can't hold New York."

"Of course he can't; but he can hold all the up-country," responded the skipper courageously. "It's goin' to be a long fight, and I tell ye what — the liberties of America won't never be safe ontil we are able to meet our enemies on the sea. We've got to have a navy!"

"Ugh!" said Up-na-tan. "Get *Noank*. Get all big gun. Kill a heap."

CHAPTER X.

THE LOST BATTLE.

THE week following the arrival of the British fleet and army was a terribly excited time for the people of the city of New York. They knew that thirty-seven men-of-war had been counted, with four hundred transport ships, and that these were said to carry thirty-five thousand soldiers, British and Hessians. Day after day the ferryboats and all the roads leading away from the city were full of men and women on foot, and of wagons loaded with household goods, and army men said there was less danger of a famine now that three quarters of the citizens had left Manhattan Island.

If only a quarter of them remained, however, it looked as if they must all have gathered in Lower Broadway, on the afternoon of the ninth of July, 1776.

If it was a mob, it was made up of the best people as well as the worst. It contained as many women as men, and more boys than either; but there were not many soldiers in it, for General Washington was trying to enforce discipline, and a mob was no place for soldiers.

During two whole days there had been great news in the city. The Continental Congress at Philadelphia, had adopted the Declaration of Independence, on the Fourth of July, and as yet nobody knew what the province of New York was going to do about it. Even Washington had said nothing, for he was not the New York legislature, and had no power to speak for it.

The exciting question in the minds of the mob seemed to be :

" If we are free why don't we say so ? Isn't New York going to declare its independence ? What are we going to do ? "

It was a perfectly free public meeting, without any chairman. Anybody could speak, and so almost everybody seemed to be saying something. It had gathered there, probably, because the Common was now occupied by camps, and the Bowling Green was about the best open space left.

Right in the middle of the Green stood the great leaden statue of King George the Third, on horseback, as silent as ever, and in front of it stood Guert Ten Eyck, looking up and thinking :

" He isn't king any more in America ! "

Perhaps a great many others were thinking or were

saying something of that kind; but, suddenly, an excited and tremulous, but very clear and courageous girlish voice called out to him:

"Guert, if we are really free, why don't they pull down the king?"

He turned for one quick glance at Maud, leaning forward and pointing, and he heard a tall woman at her side say:

"Thee is right, Maud. Thy country has no more use for kings."

"Hurrah!" shouted Guert. "Down with him!"

A hundred voices echoed, "Pull him down!" and a hundred pairs of strong arms were ready to do the work. Ladders, ropes, pulleys, came quickly. There was wild cheering, eager tugging at ropes and prying with levers, and then over rolled the statue, horse and man.

"Cut him up!" shouted somebody, and sharp axes fell rapidly upon the soft metal, but Rachel very bitterly remarked:

"Thee can destroy him more easily because he is hollow."

"And what'll we do with him now?" loudly demanded one of the axe men.

"Send all the lead to the bullet factory at my uncle's house in Litchfield," shouted Maud, and the answer came:

"That's what we'll do, right away. Load it on a wagon and send it."

So it was done, but no one was there who could say beforehand that the Litchfield women would mold over forty thousand bullets out of the leaden king and his horse, or that a tally would be kept of the battle work done with those bullets, until over four hundred of them were known to have found a fatal mark.

"Maud," said Rachel, at last, "we have seen them pull down the king. We will go home. How does thee feel, now thee has no king?"

"Pretty well, thank you," said Maud. "I don't believe we ever had one. What's the use of a king, anyhow?"

It was more than a week afterwards that the gilded "king's arms" were taken out of the Council Chamber, in the City Hall, and were publicly burned on Wall Street, while the Declaration of Independence was officially proclaimed.

All the while, however, Washington knew that the Declaration would act as a strong stimulus upon the British commanders, and he was doing all he could to be ready for them. He had enough to do, and so had Guert's scout-boat, and the reason why this so often contained four instead of three was because of Nathan Hale's skill with a pencil and paper. He could make maps and pictures which reported the doings of the enemy in a way that could be understood at headquarters.

"I'm trying to learn how," said Guert to Maud,

one day, "but you can't tell what my pictures stand for. You can read his, though. He knows pretty much everything."

"And he's the handsomest man in our army," replied Maud. "And he's always so pleasant to everybody."

He was a man whom everybody liked, at all events, and Guert saw nothing to wonder at in the increasing devotion manifested for him by Co-co and Up-na-tan. Their faces would brighten when they looked into his for the kindly greeting he always gave them, and in the boat they watched for his orders as if he had been a superior being. So he was, beyond doubt, and Guert found himself now and then thinking :

"Don't I wish I could be a man like Nathan Hale? General Washington and all of them trust him. He'll be a general himself, some day. Guess I wouldn't make much of a general."

As yet he was nothing but a boy in a boat ; but on the twenty-second of August he was a pretty proud boy, for he and his squad brought in the first news that the British army was landing at several places on the shore of Long Island, and that so the long-expected struggle was at hand. Other scouts came hurrying in with the same report, and somehow it seemed to wake up the people and make them more cheerful. There had been a suspense that had depressed them, and now it would soon be over.

"There'll be an awful fight," said Guert to his crew; "but the British can't get over the Brooklyn forts."

"Heap gun," said Up-na-tan.

"Yo, yo!" chuckled Co-co. "Wish dah was moah. Kill 'em all."

Their confidence was so complete in the strength of the works on the Brooklyn heights that Guert was utterly astonished when he remarked to Captain Hale:

"They can't take 'em," and when Hale replied:

"If the redcoats beat us in the field and break through within sight of those works, I'm afraid we will have to get out of them."

Guert went away over to Brooklyn, after that, for another look at the works. They did indeed seem strong. There were so many cannon, too, and some of them were large, and there were thousands of brave men. What chance would an enemy have? Why, he felt as if he himself could rest a bell-muzzled ducking-gun across one of those ramparts and kill any number of redcoats, just as the boys did at Bunker Hill. He could not at all understand what Hale meant; but he was soon to know more about war, and so was Up-na-tan.

The old chief seemed to be all the while in a high state of war spirits. He openly exulted as day after day went by, since the redcoats landed on Long Island, without their doing anything more. He did not really care how much land they might capture, over there, so long as the more precious island that he owned was protected.

Just about sunrise of the twenty-seventh of August, however, he and Co-co and Guert came in from a night excursion down the harbor and went at once to Washington's quarters.

"We must see Colonel Burr," said Guert hastily, to the officer on duty.

"You can't," was the reply. "He has been transferred to General Putnam's staff."

"Ugh!" sharply exclaimed Up-na-tan. "No care for Burr. No time for go to see Hale. You go, now! Tell great chief, me here, Up-na-tan. King ship come up from Lower Bay. Big ship heap move. All come shoot Manhattan Island. Tell now! No wait for Burr."

"No, indeed!" almost shouted the officer. "General Washington must know at once."

Away he went and he quickly came again, but Guert was not present when Up-na-tan gave the rest of his report to the general. He only knew how important it was considered when Washington came out and sprang upon his horse and galloped away to the Brooklyn ferry. He heard him say to an officer he left behind:

"See Putnam at once! If Sullivan should be defeated" —

That was all; but Up-na-tan's face had lost its angry cloud, and he said to Guert, as if speaking of having a good time:

"Come! Go to fort. See big fight. Great chief gone to see. King ship no come till tide turns. Ugh!"

He only half-suppressed a war-whoop, and he and Co-co and Guert hurried to their own boat, and pulled over to the Brooklyn side.

"Great gun," said Up-na-tan, as they rowed along. "No fort gun. Hark! Way over. Ugh!"

Boom, boom, boom, came the increasing sound of heavy artillery, and a chilly feeling crept over Guert as he understood that it was coming nearer.

Up the bank they clambered, leaving their boat concealed, and they hurried on toward the works on the heights, but Washington was there before them. They saw him, shortly after they reached the ramparts, whose strength they had so strongly believed in. He stood, bareheaded, on the highest point he could reach, and he watched through a telescope the long lines of smoke that were steadily pressing nearer from the eastward.

"It's the battle," groaned Guert. "They are driving our men! We are being beaten!"

"Heap gun here," said Up-na-tan, hugging with one long arm a huge iron thirty-two pounder by which he had taken his position. "Kill heap lobster."

Nothing could shake his confidence in large cannon; but Guert could see that Washington was learning terrible news through his telescope. Moreover, one after another, officers and men whose faces told how sick at heart they were, came riding breathlessly in with reports for the Commander-in-Chief.

There had been something like a surprise made by the British army, in spite of all the precautions he had taken, and Sullivan's force had been outflanked. They were terribly outnumbered, too, and it made little difference that they were fighting so bravely. Nearer and nearer drifted the broken battle, and now Guert himself could see it plainly.

"I couldn't be of any use," he gasped. "All the men there are trying to get away."

So they were, and fighting for it rather than running, for Guert heard General Washington exclaim, as he watched them from the rampart:

"Great God! what brave fellows I must lose this day!"

Nearer, nearer, and many had already reached the forts, and more were being helped to do so in a way that Washington was watching closely.

Guert saw that all was not confusion in that retreat of beaten men. He saw that red-uniformed pursuers recoiled from the persistent work of one battery of field artillery and the brave men who rallied with it to protect the American rear.

Cool, steady, in the face of almost certain death or capture, under the command, it seemed, of the shortest, slightest man among them; and Guert saw the general's face flush with admiration.

"General Greene spoke to me about him," he said, but Guert exclaimed:

"Why, that's Aleck Hamilton! I hope he'll get in safe. Nathan Hale is with him! Here they come!"

So they did, and Alexander Hamilton's after career was changed for him by the manner in which he brought in the American rear after the battle of Long Island. There was not a great deal to bring in, for over three thousand men had been lost, including prisoners. It was true that the British had also suffered heavy losses, and that the reinforcements Washington had sent for were coming over the East River from New York rapidly; but the general was thinking also of Up-na-tan's news about the British fleet. What if the ships-of-war should get in between him and Manhattan Island? Then he would be caught in a kind of trap, and would have to surrender.

Guert had seen a battle. That is, he had seen the end of one and the defeat of the best soldiers of America by the best soldiers of England. He knew that only superior numbers had gained the day, but it was a very bitter thing to think of.

"I'll stay and help defend the fort, anyhow," he said to himself. "I can do something."

Up-na-tan did not say anything, but he evidently had determined to remain as near as possible to those large cannon which were to prevent the British from getting across the East River to capture his island.

As for Co-co, he shortly disappeared and they did not see him again until late in the evening. Then he came striding along with a good-sized basket on one arm, and when he opened it they knew that he had visited both the Ten Eyck place and Mrs. Murray's. There were cooked rations for more than a squad of three, and Co-co reported gleefully:

"Yo, yo! Guert ort to see de women. Dey was mad all ober. All say to fight lobster."

"Ugh!" said Up-na-tan. "Eat a heap. Squaw know. Ugh! Good!"

He might well say so, for there were a great many of the defenders of those works who did not get plenty to eat, in the dismay and confusion of the night after the lost battle.

When the next day came there were more American reinforcements, but it could be seen from the ramparts that the British were steadily closing in. There were further reports, too, of the movement of the men-of-war in the bay. Noon came and went, and Guert and his friends had hardly finished their luncheon when the heavier artillery of the enemy began to boom, boom, and one shot skipped over the earthwork very near them.

"They are coming!" exclaimed Guert, but something else was also coming.

Perhaps the clouds of powder-smoke had prevented him from noticing any other clouds; but the sky had been getting dark and heavy, and now there suddenly poured down sheets and torrents of warm, drenching rain. There was louder thunder than that of the artillery on either side; but it was the rain and not the thunder that stopped the work of the British and American guns.

"One of the biggest rains I ever saw," Guert remarked, as he stood up in it and could see nothing a rod away.

"I think the British attack has been drowned out," said a voice behind him that he knew. "But this will be Washington's opportunity. Hamilton, we can't move these heavy guns through the mud."

"We shall have to leave some of them," was replied mournfully. "This is awful, Captain Hale. We haven't a gun to spare."

"The boats and sloops are gathering fast," said Hale. "It'll be touch and go; but I hope we can save the army."

"Save the army?" exclaimed Guert. "Why, are we going to give up these forts?"

"That's what we must do," said Hale. "But we must get away before those fellows out there know we are going."

"The last man over will take the greatest risk," remarked Hamilton.

Guert's heart was rising to his throat with grief, but he said:

"I won't go till the last man does."

"That's just what I want your squad to do," said Hale. "Stay right here and watch. I'll see that your boat is left where you can find it."

"Ugh!" grunted Up-na-tan. "Chief stay by gun."

Guert could not quite do that, for he made more than one hurried excursion back and forth, in the pouring rain, to find out what was going on. He saw a great deal, too, as he came and went, for all sorts of craft were gathering in the East River to ferry the army, and regiment after regiment was marched down, as evening came on, and was gloomily boated over. Horses went, and cannon, and wagon-loads of all kinds of stores, as well as men; and part of the works began to wear a disarmed and deserted look. Hours went by, and the rain ceased; but it was followed by a dense blue fog, through which nobody could tell whether or not the British were coming.

Not for one moment did Up-na-tan desert his "long thirty-two," and when men came along with spikes and hammers, to "spike" the guns to be left behind, he managed to save his favorite untouched.

"Ugh!" he said. "Shoot a heap, by and by."

Guert and Co-co had nothing to do but to stand or walk around, and to peer through the dense darkness, and to listen. It grew dreadfully silent as well as dark, after awhile, for the army had gone.

"It must be about time for us to go too," thought Guert. "We are not of any earthly use here."

He did not know that, and he did not know that it was now midnight.

"Dark as a pocket," he was saying, when he heard a slight clicking sound, near him.

"Up-na-tan is lighting his pipe? He'd smoke at any time," he thought; but just then a long, shrill, defiant war-whoop rang out through the black night, and, a second later, it was followed by the roaring report of Up-na-tan's big gun.

"Ugh!" said the red man. "Up-na-tan go now. Hope kill. Come!"

Away over in the British lines an officer remarked:

"Do you hear that? The rebels are on the alert. If we had tried a right attack, they would have been ready for us. We will wait until to-morrow."

Guert was a very tired and heavy-hearted boy when he plodded on through the mud with Up-na-tan and Co-co. All the works seemed empty; but they soon found that all the army was not safe in New York. There was a great deal yet to do, and all that was left would be at the mercy of a sudden attack.

The boats were very busy, and Guert went over and

back in one of them. When he left the Brooklyn side, he could hardly see, through the fog, the length of the boat; but when its prow touched the New York shore he stepped out, exclaiming:

"Fog? No; it's all clear on this side. It's the brightest moonlight I ever saw. It doesn't do the British any good, though. It's shining for our army."

Back he went. Only a little later he stood on the Brooklyn beach, near the ferry stairs, and heard a man say: "Come, General. This is the last boat. The army is safe."

"That's Washington," thought Guert, as he looked at the tall, erect form standing silently on the ferry stairs, but at that moment he saw Up-na-tan step forward.

"Ugh!" said the Manhattan, almost as if giving an order. "Go! No stay, be caught. Up-na-tan stay. King men find him. Keep him one day. Come to great chief. See what redcoat do. Keep little boat. So, so, Up-na-tan!"

Washington held out a hand almost impulsively, as he replied:

"Stay, my brave fellow. It will be a great service. Can you get away to-morrow?"

"No tell," said Up-na-tan. "S'pose any Iroquois see him, lose 'calp."

"There are none of them here, I think," said the General. "I will go now."

He stepped into the ferryboat and was rowed away, but not before Up-na-tan had taken Guert's and Co-co's muskets from them and handed them to the boatmen.

"No good," he said. "No shoot now. Guert Dutch boy. Talk Dutch. B'long to old king. No rebel. Up-na-tan Mohawk. Co-co b'long to Lancey. Come!"

The small boat left with them was pulled ashore, and as they once more climbed the steep bank, Guert began to understand the idea of Up-na-tan, and knew that they three were spies.

He had a great deal to think of during several dark hours. Even after the sun arose, there was fog on the Brooklyn shore. He did not know that under cover of it, the British ships were slowly feeling their way up the harbor, but he felt as if he and his squad were left alone to face the whole British army under Sir William Howe.

It was still very early that morning, when Rachel Tarns stood grimly in the doorway of the Ten Eyck farmhouse, demanding:

"Has Guert come home, Anneke?"

"Guert?" exclaimed his mother. "O, Rachel! Guert is in the army. He is with Washington."

"Thee is a brave, good woman," said Rachel earnestly. "I have no sons to give him. It is just as well. They would be Quakers. What the country wants, just now, is not men of peace. I hope Guert will not fall into the hands of the enemy."

Nevertheless, that was just what he had done, before seven o'clock, and he and his friends were standing among a group of British officers, answering surprised and angry questions.

"Rebel get away in dark," reported Up-na-tan, telling pretty minutely how Washington had managed his retreat, and adding, "Rebel take all boat, all 'cooner, all sloop. Take boat from poor ole Indian. 'Teal him, too. Make him work all night."

"Make poor ole niggah work," said Co-co dolefully. "'Teal him. 'Teal Dutch boy. Make him work"—

"What a looking lot of crows they are, too," said one of the officers. "They may have staid behind to steal what they could to pay for their work."

Guert had already replied to them and to his friends, in good Dutch, and all the mud on his soaked clothing helped the story of Up-na-tan.

"Anyhow," remarked the officer who had questioned them, "they have told us what we wanted to know. Mr. Washington has done one of the greatest things on record, and we have missed capturing the rebel army."

"General Cornwallis, shall we shoot these fellows?" asked a red-faced major. "We can't let them go."

"Yes, we can," replied Cornwallis. "They are not worth shooting. Besides, they have been the best

"GENERAL CORNWALLIS, SHALL WE SHOOT THESE FELLOWS?"

kind of spies for us, and they can't do us any harm. They can't even get away without a boat."

Guert heard him, as he and his friends walked away, and a minute or so later he said something in Dutch to Co-co. The Ashantee spoke at once to Up-na-tan in Spanish and was answered, after a swift glance around for listeners :

"Ugh! Good! Heap swim when dark come. See all can now. Hear a heap. Count ship. Tell great chief what king men do. Ugh!"

Guert understood that to be precisely what Washington wished them to do, but he had a dolefully hard time that day. Before it ended he found himself talking very good English, in reply to some of the soldiers who continually questioned him concerning the escape of Washington's army. He found, too, that his Dutch was an altogether different tongue from the German talked by the Hessian troops who had come over to aid in putting down the rebel subjects of the English king.

Up-na-tan felt very sure that there had been no Iroquois among the passengers of the fleet. He strolled listlessly about like a fellow who had nothing in the world to do, and who cared less than nothing for soldiers and war. Co-co went with him, limping dreadfully as to his left leg, and there was no danger that a white-headed, worthless old black man, crippled with rheumatism, would be pressed into any part of the

British army or navy. There might have been some question about Guert's security from permanent duties, if it had not been a time when everybody was thinking about something else. At all events, the long hours wore away and the three spies were entirely safe when the sun went down. The last light found them on the beach of the East River, looking across the narrowest part of its long, wide channel, through which the tide was then pouring. One after another several ships of war had gone by, to take up positions where their guns commanded the eastern shore of Manhattan Island.

"There goes the old *Asia*," said Guert. "She has watched New York ever so long."

"Ugh!" exclaimed Up-na-tan excitedly. "Look! *Noank*. Heap gun!"

"That's so!" eagerly responded Guert. "And Skipper Avery's in the city. I saw him, day before yesterday."

"Catch her, dis time," said Co-co. "Dey's goin' to Kip's Bay. Find 'em dah, suah!"

He seemed to have no idea but what the *Noank* was going up the East River for American rather than British purposes, but his feelings were not stirred up as were those of Up-na-tan. The old pirate looked more like one than ever as he glared after the *Asia* and the squad of smaller craft she was guarding, and he muttered fierce words in more tongues than one.

He could be patient, however, for he was an Indian, and they all waited for the darkness.

There were sentries stationed all along the shore; but the three scouts had no trouble in evading them, for every redcoat was watching the New York side of the water and not his own.

"Now!" hissed Up-na-tan. "Guert follow. Let tide carry him."

In an instant they were in the water, as silently as so many eels, and the tide swept them on as it had swept the ships, only that the three spies were also swimming vigorously across its current. It was not at all a difficult feat for three good swimmers, used to salt water.

There would have been little more to speak of than a good bath, if it had not been for the vigilant night-watch on the deck of the *Merlin*, as she lay at anchor.

They were keeping a keen lookout, and they did not fail to notice something or other suspicious on the water, borne rapidly past the ship. They hailed it, of course, but there was no answer. They hailed again, and then Guert heard a quick command:

"Fire!"

It was followed by a rattle of musketry, and the balls hissed near him, as they struck the water. There was no answering shot. Nothing but the mocking war-whoop of Up-na-tan, and before a boat could be lowered and sent in pursuit of them, the three escaped spies had gained the shore and were pushing on toward the tangled swamp below Bowery Lane.

"Guert hit?" asked Up-na-tan.

"No," began Guert; but the old Indian at once pushed up his left shirt sleeve, for he wore no coat, and for the first time he was aware that one of the bullets had grazed his left arm.

"Ugh! Good!" exclaimed Up-na-tan. "Now Guert soldier! Brave!"

"Yo, yo!" laughed Co-co. "Leetle blood come. Jus' nuff to show pretty girl. Yo!"

And the fact was that Guert had never before felt such a thrill of pride as he did over the scratch on his arm that testified to the peril through which he had swam the East River.

CHAPTER XI.

CUTTING OUT THE NOANK.

"SO thee has been wounded in battle," said Rachel Tarns, as she looked down into Guert's face the next morning.

"No, I wasn't," said Guert cheerfully. "I was wounded in the water. It won't amount to anything."

His mother sat by her loom, but she was not weaving. She had turned to look at Guert, and her eyes agreed with Rachel, whose next remark was:

"Thee looks pretty well, with thy arm in a sling. Thy foolish mother is even proud of thee."

He did not look badly, now that the mud was washed from his face and hands, and he was dressed in a new suit of homespun.

His arm was not troubling him, but he had an idea that the sling it rested in was something like epaulets. He had had a long sleep after reaching home, and now he felt like having another, but it did not seem exactly the time to be in bed.

It seemed less so an hour later when he was telling Maud Wolcott and Mrs. Murray all he knew or had seen of General Washington's wonderful retreat from Long Island. They came over to hear about it as soon as Rachel told them of Guert's return.

"Guert," said Maud, at last, "have we got to give up New York?"

"Captain Hale said so, when we reported to him last night," said Guert. "They are too strong for us. Some of our men are sick, too, and some are going home."

"I'm going home as soon as I can," replied Maud; "but there isn't any chance to get away, just now."

"And mother," said Guert, "means to go away up the Hudson to live at Mr. Van Wart's. She won't stay in New York if our army leaves it."

"I can't get away," said Mrs. Murray. "Perhaps I'd better stay. I can't do anything anywhere else, but I wish I could go to France — or to China. It's terrible!"

"Guert!" suddenly exclaimed Maud. "There's Up-na-tan at the gate."

He was there with his inseparable black ally, and not many minutes later, they and Guert were on their way to the lower part of the city. It was indeed feeling pretty low that day, for a great deal of it was within cannon shot of British men-of-war. It was busy, too, for the streets were full of wagons. Some of these were carrying away people and household goods, and some were loaded with army stores of all kinds that were going to places of greater safety, away up the island, or even beyond it. There were not wagons enough, however, and too many of them carried sick soldiers. It was a very blue time.

Guert saw it all; but he and his friends were on a hunt, and it was only after many inquiries that they found that Knowlton's regiment, to which Captain Hale belonged, was away up the East River, on the shore of Kip's Bay, and that they must trudge back again.

"Anyhow," said Guert, "that's where Skipper Avery will be, with the other New London men."

"Find him!" exclaimed Up-na-tan. "Go and get *Noank*. Want gun. Make Kidd ship."

Very plain was his understanding that there was little or no difference between one kind of man-of-war and another. Captain Kidd had been a great chief on the sea, and as good a war captain as he cared to sail under. He now thought well of Skipper Avery, and Co-co remarked:

"I see de *Noank*. Seen her all ober. Mighty 'trong 'cooner. Catch any boat I ebber seen. Run away, too."

They were old seamen, and they knew what they were saying. The staunchly built New London whaling schooner had been planned for rough seas, and was fit to carry guns. She was just the vessel to be turned into a privateer; that is, into the kind of cruiser that the British were calling "Yankee pirates."

Guert could hear all they had to say, and he understood a great deal of it, but his spirits were away down. Up-na-tan might be even more cheerful, because all the American army was now guarding his own island for him, and Co-co could laugh at any time; but everybody they met wore a gloomy face, and it was of no use for the sun to shine so brightly. It was something like a surprise, therefore, when they at last reached Knowlton's camp and Captain Hale came out to meet them, for his face was as brave and confident as if there had been no defeat, or as if he were looking forward only to victory.

"Hurrah for you, Guert!" he said, and so said Skipper Avery, just behind him. "It was a plucky thing for you to do."

"'Twasn't much," replied Guert. "I've swum further than that. I can move my arm pretty well, too."

"That'll heal right over," said the skipper; "but, I tell ye what, I know just where the *Asia* is, and the *Noank*. They're anchored not more'n two hundred yards apart. I'm goin' to git her back, though, sure as guns!"

"So, so!" exclaimed the Manhattan. "Get *Noank*. Get heap big gun. When go?"

"I'm picking up the right sort of men," said the skipper; "but what we want is a couple of whaleboats. Soon's I can git them, we'll pitch right in."

They talked and they planned, and all the while Guert found himself watching the bright face of the captain. It seemed to do him good.

"Up-na-tan is brave," he thought; "so is Co-co. They're not afraid of anything. But they're not as brave as Nathan Hale. I wonder if Aleck Hamilton's as brave as he is. General Washington is. I don't believe I am."

He felt a great deal less so when he went away, but his spirits went down again, during several days that followed. Everybody knew that there were negotiations going on between Congress and Washington and the British commanders, and there were dark rumors that the Americans were going to give it all up, because they had been beaten so badly.

"I guess they won't," said Guert to his mother. "They won't if Washington's as brave as Nathan Hale is."

"Of course they won't," said his mother. "Let me fix up your arm before you go out. You don't need the sling any more."

He was willing to give up his ornament, for that night at least, considering what might be before him, and he was not marked as a wounded man when he went out. He told his mother:

"We are going out in the boat and the captain is going with us. So is the skipper."

"I'm glad of that," she said. "They won't do anything foolish or too risky."

Perhaps they did not, but when Guert joined them, after a long evening walk, they and a score of other men were gathered at the head of one of the narrow inlets among the rushes of the Harlem swamps. They were all armed to the teeth, for every man wore a cutlass as well as belt pistols, and they looked like buccaneers, for none of them were in uniform excepting Captain Hale. For all that, they were carefully picked New England seamen, of the toughest, hardiest kind, and they were now taking their places in a pair of long, graceful-looking whale-boats.

"It's going to be a pretty dark night," said Guert. "They can't see us."

"Just what we want," said Hale. "We're all right, if the *Noank* is anchored by a hempen cable. See that Indian! A good deal depends on him."

Guert had already been watching the movements of Up-na-tan. The old pirate wore no cutlass, but he seemed to think of making a razor out of his long-knife, by the way he stropped it on his leggings and tried its edge again and again.

Out through the dark and winding inlet slipped the two whale-boats, and when they were in open water, and the crews took to the oars, all was as silent as ever, for the rowlocks were muffled and the blades were dipped as if splashing might be dangerous. It was indeed dark. It was just the night for two such boats to glide along like ghosts over the quiet water.

"We shall get there just as the tide begins to run well," remarked Hale, "and then it'll be quick work, live or die."

"We've passed more than one boat," said Guert; "not of our side, I guess."

"Navy patrol boats," replied Hale. "They must have mistaken us for some of the same sort."

"We're strong enough to capter any patrol boat," growled Skipper Avery, "but I'm right down glad we didn't hev to dew it."

"Ugh!" exclaimed Up-na-tan. "Hale wait for old chief. So!"

Guert heard no signal, but both of the whale-boats were instantly still. He was looking at the head of Up-na-tan, for that was all of him that could be seen above the waves into which he had slipped, over the side of the boat.

"The *Noank* lies out yonder," said Hale. "I didn't think we were so near."

Near or far, it was a trial of any one's nerves to sit there and wait, in the midst of unknown danger.

"I guess I'm not brave enough to stand it long," thought Guert. "I want to be doing something. Wish I knew what Up-na-tan is doing."

At first he was only swimming, with a strong, steady stroke, but it carried him rapidly along, and in a few minutes a great black mass of shadow began to show a little ahead of him.

"Ugh!" he grunted. "*Asia.* No want big ship. Where *Noank?* Ugh!"

Again he swam fast, and the tide aided him, and in a little while he had no need to swim, for he could hold by one hand to a thick rope. It was the cable that held the *Noank* at her anchor, and Up-na-tan was cutting at it with his very sharp knife.

It was the last thing that anybody on board the schooner could have been expecting, for the Americans had no navy, and their defeated army on the shore had no means of harming the fleet or any vessels under its powerful protection. It looked very much, however, if a seaman had been studying the deck and spars of the *Noank*, as if she were only waiting for orders to raise her sails and go to some other anchorage.

Saw, saw, cut, cut, worked the knife at the cable; but it made no noise, and the water that gurgled around the hull of the *Noank* was enough to drown the low, hard breathing of the last of the Manhattans.

The vessel made just a little lurch when the last hempen strand was suddenly severed. Then she was swept away by the rushing tide, and the watchers on her deck heard a shrill whistle in her wake, and what seemed an answer, out in the darkness near them.

They were few in number. Not by any means all of them were armed. They were utterly taken by surprise, moreover, and just as a tall figure, brandishing a long knife, clambered over the stern and rushed toward the wheel as if he intended to steer her, the hushed plash of muffled oars came quickly on both sides of her, grappling irons were thrown on board, and these were followed by a rush of stalwart men.

"Silence, for your lives!" was the hoarse command of the first voice they heard, and it was followed by:

"If any man fires a shot, cut him down and throw him overboard!"

They were hopelessly outnumbered, and the only regular naval officer on board was asleep in his hammock below. Not one of them was willing to be killed, just for the privilege of firing a gun, and so they quietly surrendered, while Captain Hale's men swiftly hoisted the sails of the schooner. In a few minutes more she was speeding away through the shadows, while a British naval officer on the deck of the *Merlin* was remarking:

"Moved? has she? All right. I knew she was going to, but she got her orders quicker than I thought she would."

Captain Hale and his men had therefore captured the *Noank* with little more noise than would have naturally been made by a bungling crew in heaving her anchor and getting her under sail. The anchor had been left behind, however, and her very full cargo of provisions was to be delivered to the American army messes. They were all in need of just such supplies, for the Continentals were made low spirited by lack of food as well as by their defeat in battle.

No other men on board of the *Noank*, or anywhere else, were more anxious to get her rations out of her than were Skipper Avery, Up-na-tan, Guert and Co-co.

They had the hearty sympathy of Hale, and were promised that as soon as the mouth of the Bronx River could be reached the cargo should be out in a twinkling.

"Ugh!" replied Up-na-tan, with eyes that glittered triumphantly. "Get up heap gun! Make Kidd ship! Go heap fight! So, so, Up-na-tan!"

"I won't go home till I see every gun there is down there," said Guert, as he peered down the open hatchway into the hold. "I want to know what the skipper bought with that money."

"Ship guns, mostly," said Hale, standing by him; "one field battery. Our men can arm and fit out the *Noank* right here, and then she had better put to sea at once, or some of these British men-of-war may find her."

There was danger of that, although there was a kind of truce between the armies, while the Admiral Lord Howe tried his best to convince General Washington and Congress that they had better give it up. The General had his hands full, but Guert would have had very little to do if it had not been for the hold of the *Noank*.

What a treasure chamber that deep hole was, and what wonders of war came up, after they got out the provisions and began to stir the ballast. Guert found that he and his friends took only a small amount of interest in any cannon that were to go ashore; but Up-na-tan danced a war-dance of joyful whooping when a long, brass eighteen-pounder was hoisted on deck, followed by all the fixings for mounting it as a swivel, to swing around and shoot in any direction. Then there came up first-class brass "sixes," to serve as broadside guns, three on a side, making the *Noank* a pretty well-armed privateer, and her authority for that kind of cruising had already been given her, so that her skipper was now a kind of sea captain.

"Ugh!" remarked Up-na-tan. "Plenty powder. Heap shot. Heap musket, pistol, cutlass, pike, knife, tomahawk. Kill a heap!"

It was indeed a most piratical looking lot of weapons, and it told what good use the skipper had made of the money.

"Prizes?" exclaimed Captain Avery. "Why, Hale, we shall scoop in any number of 'em. I know where to go."

They were not ready for sailing, yet, however, and

Captain Hale sent Guert home, telling him that he would soon have work for the squad of scouts. That seemed to suit Up-na-tan and Co-co, too, and they also went ashore.

Nobody knew exactly how the truce ended; but on the morning of the fifteenth of September, the families living near the fork of the Bowery Lane and the Bloomingdale Road were startled by the roar of heavy guns. Quite a number of the women, at least, seemed to be taken with a sudden impulse that carried them hurriedly to Mrs. Ten Eyck's.

"It sounds as if it were over at Kip's Bay," said Mrs. Murray to Maud.

"Guert'll know what it is," replied Maud.

"I do so hope he's at home. We didn't get a bit of news, all day yesterday."

They did not get any now, for each new arrival had to be told:

"Guert is down town. He says our army is to leave New York. Captain Hale told him."

"The British are coming!" exclaimed Maud. "How I wish I could go and see something! If I had a horse, to ride!"

"I sent mine to Westchester, with a load, two days ago," said Mrs. Murray. "You couldn't ride them, anyhow."

"I can fix thee," said Rachel Tarns. "I told Israel Putnam's wife that her husband might have my horses to pull his cannon away; but thee can go and get the pony Aaron Burr left in my stable, when he stole my gray mare. It is good enough for thee, and nobody will steal it from thee."

"Good enough?" said Maud. "I guess it is. I'll get it. If I see anything to tell, I'll come right back."

She easily saddled the pony, but she was not to come right back. She set out at once at the pony's best gallop, exclaiming to herself, aloud:

"Hear the cannons! What an awful roar they make. I don't care. I want to see a battle. If there's one there, I'll see how it looks."

She had a pretty sharp ride to make before she reached the high ground that sloped down toward the bay. It was indeed worth seeing, then. Out upon the water was a long line of British war-ships, their tall masts standing up through the clouds of smoke which arose from their repeated broadsides, aimed at the American earthworks along the shore. Nearing the shore were scores and scores of boats, full of red-coated soldiers, and already what seemed to Maud an army of these had landed and formed on the beach, and were marching gallantly forward.

There was no answering cannonade from the Americans, except for a short time, at the first. Then it was shown how defeat and sickness and hunger could take the courage out of brave men; for some of the best soldiers in the Continental Army gave up and began to retreat, without orders and without trying to stop the advance of the enemy.

"What," said Maud, "don't our men mean to fight them? I would, if I were a man. But the British are marching splendidly! There, the ships have stopped firing. Oh! there's General Washington."

Her pony had carried her forward and, in her excitement, she did not know that she was in danger, nor did she pay any attention to the buzz of British bullets over her head. She was a girl soldier, full of the fire of battle, and now she saw that the General was boiling over with fight and with anger at his retreating men. She could hear that he was storming at them, urging them to turn and face the enemy, but she could not get the exact words he was saying. She saw him even draw a pistol and snap it at his own men; but fortunately it was empty, and did not hurt anybody. The British advance was very near, but Maud's pony took another canter, and just then she saw the General, after swinging his hat, hoarsely shouting to his men, dash it angrily on the ground. The enemy were closing up fast, the American ranks were breaking.

"They will kill him!" screamed Maud. "Or they will take him prisoner. There!"

She shouted again, she knew not what, for a mounted officer caught the bridle of Washington's horse and forcibly led him away, whether he would or no.

"His hat!" exclaimed Maud, for she saw a man picking it up.

Several companies of the Continentals had not broken, but were retreating in good order, exchanging volleys with the advancing British, and the commander of one of these was near Maud when she wheeled her pony.

"Captain Hale," she exclaimed, "let me carry him that hat!"

He had seen her before, for he said:

"Miss Wolcott, ride to the fort at Richmond Hill, and tell about this disgrace. Knowlton's men never broke before. Tell them to retreat. Our flank is turned."

Maud was not soldier enough to know what that meant, but she replied:

"I will; I'll ride and tell them. This is too bad."

Just then a soldier handed her the gold-laced cocked hat of the Commander-in-Chief, and she did not have to whip her pony. He must have had some war-spirit in him, from the way in which he dashed forward toward the spot where Washington had again halted, striving to rally a regiment.

He was still furiously excited, but he had recovered his dignity. She thought he looked splendid, sitting on his large black horse, bareheaded, white-faced, with quivering lips that were generally so firm, and appealing hoarsely to his men to stand for their liberties.

She could not utter a word, as she leaned forward in her saddle and delivered her prize.

Neither did he respond, as he took it and put it on, except by a low bow of perfect courtesy, and :

"Thank you, my dear young lady."

Away sprang Maud's pony, for her whip fell sharply. She knew that she was crying, right out aloud, and she had a message for the men in Richmond Hill fort.

"I'll let them know at the house, first," she thought. "Then I'll do all I can."

She hardly knew what she told them when she reached the front of Mrs. Murray's piazza. It was full of women. Even Jane De Lancey was there, and several other Tory neighbors, and their faces were bright enough when Maud said.

"The British generals are coming right down this way. I saw some of them. They want to catch our army."

She did not see a queer, sharp look in the face of Mrs. Murray, turned toward Rachel Tarns.

"Rachel," she said, "my husband is a Friend, if I am not, and I am a woman given to hospitality."

"Thee is wise, also," said Rachel. "Jane De Lancey, is thee a loyal woman? If thee is, thee will get thee ready to entertain the servants of thy king when they arrive. The day is warm and they will be in need of the best we can do for them."

"We'll give them the best luncheon," exclaimed

Mrs. Murray; and Miss De Lancey and several of her friends joined her with the greatest zeal, as she hurried her preparations.

The zeal was nearly galloped out of Maud's pony when she reached the works on Richmond Hill. It was well that she got there, however, with her news from Kip's Bay, for if there had been too little courage among the Americans there, those here were showing too much.

"Maud!" shouted a voice she knew, as her perspiring pony cantered near the outer line of breastworks. "I just came up from the city with Colonel Burr. He wants the troops here to retreat, but Hamilton and the rest say the fort must be defended."

"Nathan Hale says they'll all be taken prisoners!" shouted Maud. "We were beaten at Kip's Bay. I was there and saw our men run. It was too bad."

"Did you see the fight?" came back from Guert, but she finished her errand.

"The British are coming," she said. "They are almost at our house. You've got to be quick about it."

"That will do, Putnam," exclaimed a deep voice beyond Guert. "Form two columns. They may strike us as we go."

"If anything under heaven could delay their advance one hour," responded General Putnam, "we'd save every man."

"Maud," said Guert, "hurry home. Get out of the way of the army."

"Your mother's at our house, and lots of them," said Maud, but she wheeled her pony homeward with a sudden idea that she had a new errand, for she heard Aaron Burr saying to Guert:

"Ten Eyck, you and I know all the cross-roads. You guide Silliman's column and I'll guide Putnam's. Lead them through the lanes this side of Mrs. Murray's. If Howe's men would only halt one hour!"

"Home, home!" said Maud to herself. "I want to see Aunt Murray."

Rachel Tarns had not heard anything, but she stood on the Murray piazza and said, in a very low voice:

"Anneke, thee must not talk treason. Thee must help Sarah and me keep those men from going forward too fast in this hot sun."

Miss De Lancey and the other Tory ladies present did not hear her, for they were intently watching Stephen De Lancey as he very gracefully and proudly delivered to a brilliant group of horsemen an invitation to come into the Murray mansion for rest and refreshment.

The response was hearty indeed, for one of the horsemen remarked instantly:

"Howe, it's just the thing;" and was responded to with:

"Certainly. Cornwallis, we had better halt the troops, too. They have had a hard push in this heat. If they are to have any fighting to-day, they will do it all the better after a rest."

So the British troops were halted, and when, shortly afterwards, Maud rode in at the gate, she could glance up the road and see the long lines of dusty veterans gladly stacking their arms for a breathing spell.

"How many there are of them," she said, as she hurried on and dismounted and went into the house.

The drawing-room and the dining-room were brilliant with epaulets and uniforms.

"I won't go in with my riding habit on," thought Maud. "I must see Aunt Murray right away, though."

There was no need to send for her, and Maud's breathless errand concerning the retreating Continentals ended with:

"Aunt Sarah, General Putnam said they could get away if the British would only halt an hour."

"Maud," whispered Mrs. Murray, "don't you see the generals in there? Howe, Clinton, Cornwallis, and the colonels and staff officers? We are cooking, and we've sent to the De Lancey place for things, and they're all glad to wait till we are ready."

"O, Aunt!" exclaimed Maud, as she turned away, almost laughing; but Mrs. Murray's finger was on her lip.

It had seemed hard for brave men to give up, without a blow, works that looked so strong as did those on Richmond Hill; but they were unfinished, they were but partly armed and they were not provisioned.

So there was no use in trying to hold them, and the retreat began. It was Alexander Hamilton's duty to care for the artillery, or he might have been a good guide among the country roads and lanes of Manhattan Island. As it was, the two American columns, numbering over three thousand men, with wagons and cannon, were led by Aaron Burr and Guert Ten Eyck through winding and narrow ways toward the Hudson River side of the island. It was a safe and unmolested march, but it passed within half a mile of the Murray mansion and the British generals.

They found it cooler and pleasanter in there than it would have been on the dusty roads in the hot sun, and all the ladies were doing their parts splendidly. All was welcome and hospitality, and Rachel and Maud and Mrs. Murray talked no more treason than did Jane De Lancey herself.

Not one hour, but nearly two went by, and then Maud heard something out in the hall which made her turn to the agreeable young officer she was talking with and say: "I must excuse myself for a minute, Captain André."

In a few seconds more she was asking:

"What is it, Guert? Where are our men?"

"They are safe," whispered Guert. "We went by so near that I could see the house. Did you keep those officers here, all this time?"

"Aunt Murray did it," replied Maud triumphantly. "She and Rachel."

"Tell her she can let them go, then, just as soon as she pleases," said he. "Why, Maud, keeping those generals has stopped their whole advance. She has saved half an army!"

"And they haven't guessed it," replied Maud, with a strong tendency to clap her hands and hurrah, but at that very moment a dusty aide-de-camp was respectfully reporting something to General Sir William Howe that made the British commander's pleasant face turn fiery red.

"Marched right past us?" he exclaimed. "And we have missed them?"

"William," remarked Rachel Tarns benevolently, "thee need not worry thyself. Thee can follow Israel Putnam or George Washington some other time. Thee and thy soldiers have rested well, and thee needed rest. The day is very warm."

He looked as if it had suddenly grown warmer, but he was as polite as ever, even after he discovered that his fine luncheon had lost him an important victory.

"Maud," said Guert, out in the hall, "tell mother I'm off, but I may get back to the house to-morrow."

CHAPTER XII.

THE HERO.

"IF we are whipped for good," thought Guert, "I suppose they can set up King George again on the Bowling Green. The statue is melted up, though, and they'd have to run another."

He was feeling pretty badly, and at least one point of resemblance was coming out between him and Up-na-tan. Guert, like the old Indian, had a strong sense that Manhattan belonged to him. His family had always lived there. He was born there. It was his island and he loved it.

Both of them seemed to be losing their property, however, for the king's troops now held all of it excepting the long, narrow neck of land on its northwestern corner, between the Hudson, the Harlem and Spuyten Duyvil Creek. Here the "rebels" were still strongly fortified, but the greater part of Washington's army was above the Harlem, in Westchester county.

Up-na-tan was a man who did not tell exactly how

he felt. He seemed to find great consolation just now, in frequent visits to the *Noank*, and in seeing how the workmen progressed in turning her into a "heap Kidd ship." Guert went with him several times, but his heart was with the army rather than the navy. He preferred to remain at the camp of Knowlton's regiment, on Fort Washington heights, now and then wondering when he should get a chance to let his mother know where he was.

Only a few days went by before a chance came, and Nathan Hale brought it. He seemed in more than commonly good spirits one morning, when he said:

"Now, Guert, I want you and your squad. We've got to make a long scout, inside the British lines. General Washington wants to know exactly what they are doing."

"I'm ready," replied Guert, "and you can count on Up-na-tan and Co-co. It's just what they'd like."

"They are born and bred spies," almost laughed Hale. "You can go home and I will tell you how to help me. They can go anywhere and nobody will suspect them."

"They can hide among Up-na-tan's rocks," said Guert. "I must see mother, anyhow."

The very next night, a little punt, with four men in it, crept out of a swamp on the north shore of the Harlem and slipped across into another swamp on the south side. Then the four men slowly clambered up the bluff, by a rugged path that one of them seemed to know. After that, they kept away from all paths and made their way among the roughest, rockiest, most difficult ground to be had. They went slowly, watchfully, and in silence, until at last one of them said:

"Here we are, Captain Hale. Not more'n a mile from our house."

"I must go the rest of the way alone," said Hale. "Meet me at noon at the Freshwater Pond. I shall make two copies of every drawing or report; one for you, one for me, so that if one of them is captured the other may get to General Washington. Of course, if I am captured, I shall be shot or hung. So would you."

"I understand that," said Guert. "I could die as well as you could."

"Ugh!" said Up-na-tan. "S'pose king man kill Guert? Kill Hale? Up-na-tan kill heap lobster."

Hale strode away into the Bloomingdale Road, leaving them to their own devices.

"I'm going home," said Guert. "Will you meet me at the pond?"

"No go home," said Up-na-tan, shaking his head. "Heap lobster at house. Shut Guert up. Ask where he been."

"Guess I'd better look out," said Guert, very gloomily. "We'll find out before I go there."

Up-na-tan nodded, but turned and pointed back among the rocky ridges north of them.

"Guert 'member stone?" he said. "All there. Up-na-tan no kill yet. Guert no turn over stone till he twenty-one?"

"I'll keep my word," said Guert. "I may be killed myself."

"Ugh! No," replied Up-na-tan, as positively as if he knew. "Guert no lose 'calp. Fight a heap. Kill king man."

He did not look much like a prophet, nor did Co-co, who seemed to agree with him about Guert's future, but Guert himself was aware of a strong idea that he would get out of that scrape, somehow.

They were not to keep together, for safety's sake, and Guert was all alone when, at sunrise, he stood in the barn back of his own house, and looked through a crack to see what was going on.

There were horses in the barn, and his mother's cows were in the yard in front of it. Military saddles and bridles hung from the pegs on the wall, and a lot of muskets, carbines and sabers were stacked in one corner.

Guert stared at these, after staring a long while at the house.

"The redcoats have got us," he groaned. "But I mustn't stay here. What on earth had I better do next?"

He turned to the crack again.

"Halloo!" he exclaimed. "There's mother. She's come out to milk the cows."

She was looking well, but there was a grieved and even vindictive expression on her face as she sat down on her milking stool by one of the cows. She had hardly begun before she sprang up again, with a cry of delight, for a voice asked her in Dutch: "Mother! I'm here. Is it safe for me to come out to you?"

"O, Guert! Come," she said. "The officers they quartered on us won't be back for hours. They're away on duty. Come! Slip right into the house."

She could not even hug him until he was safely inside, but then he found out how anxious she had been about him. He told the greater part of his own story while he was eating the best breakfast he had had in two weeks.

"If Captain Hale finds anything," he said, at last, "one of us three can get back through the lines with it."

She did not discourage him. Nothing but a quiver in her lip told how well she understood the danger he was in.

"Go, now," she said. "You'd be safer at Mrs. Murray's. What a hero Nathan Hale is! I do hope he won't be caught."

"He won't unless some one sees him that knows him," said Guert; "some Tory."

"Everybody knows you," she said; "but then you're not really a soldier."

"No," replied Guert; "I tell you what, it's worth something to be only a boy, just now; but I don't want to answer any questions."

So he walked quietly away down the road, toward the business part of the island which the British had taken from him and Up-na-tan.

The greater part of General Howe's army was still over on Long Island. Some of it was on Staten Island. The British troops in New York were nearly all away up above the town, posted in front of the American lines. The city part of Manhattan Island, therefore, was only very strongly garrisoned, and Guert was surprised to see that there was even an appearance of business. He walked hither and thither and no one molested him, but he saw a great deal, and at last he remarked:

"I guess there won't be much going to meeting on Sundays. About all the churches have been turned into prisons to keep our soldiers in. They're packed and jammed full, too. They must be awful places to be cooped up in, with the weather as hot as this is."

He could only faintly guess how very awful those prisons must be, and, as noon drew near and passed, and for some time afterwards, he loitered along the shore of the Freshwater Pond.

"I used to fish there when I was a boy," he said

to himself. "I'm pretty near sixteen, now. I s'pose I shall never fish there again."

He was feeling very old and very blue, but he saw another man coming along and he waited for him. He was a tall, strong-looking young man, very shabbily dressed. Anybody would have known at once, that he was a kind of country schoolmaster, from somewhere in New England. There was nobody else within hearing when he stopped and spoke to Guert.

"I've seen everything there is any need of seeing about New York," he said. "It's been sharp work, but I've done it. Those are your report papers, and they will tell General Washington a great deal."

"I'll see that he gets them," said Guert, as he put a thin packet away in behind his waist, so that his belt held it.

"Don't try it until I give you more of another kind," said Hale. "I'm going over to scout the camps and works on Long Island. There's a sloop to sail for New London to-morrow morning, and the skipper's one of our men. I can go on her, if they don't catch me, and be put ashore on the coast above the Harlem. You'd better meet me at Murray's wharf just before she sails. I'll hand you something and you'll know what to do with it. I must go, now."

"I shall sleep down there in the swamp to-night," said Guert. "I can find a camp among the bushes."

Away walked the shabby schoolmaster on his dangerous errand, and Guert looked after him, thinking:

"Have I seen all I could see? I'll go down along the wharves to the Battery, and know all I can about the ships and what people are doing."

There were a great many loiterers, and the British commanders saw no reason for keeping a close watch on them. Over among their Long Island camps they were even more secure and careless, for there was no danger there from anything Mr. Washington's ragged rebels could do.

The swamp, south of the Bowery Lane and east of Broadway, was a pretty dry place, for a long drought had followed the rainstorm which had helped Washington to escape, after the battle of Long Island. The grass and bushes looked withered. In fact, Guert had hardly ever seen his city itself look so dry and parched.

"Dry as tinder," he said to himself, as he lay down among some comfortable soft grass and was ready to go to sleep. "I told them where to find me."

Perhaps it was as well that he had done so, for he had been very tired and he slumbered soundly until he was awakened by a shake, and heard:

"Ugh! Guert come. Sun up. Get out of swamp. Time to go."

"I'm ready," said Guert, standing and stretching himself. "Halloo, Co-co!"

"Yo, yo!" chuckled the Ashantee. "Walk right along, now. Hab some breakfuss?"

He was glad enough that they had brought him something to eat from their own night hiding-place at Mom Van Boom's; but he had to take his breakfast as they hurried along on their way toward Murray's wharf, up the East River.

When they drew nearer, they could see that there were guards posted on the wharf and that people who came or went were closely looked at. Some of them were spoken to, and some were even ordered away.

"Ugh!" said Up-na-tan. "'Top here. Chief come. Look!"

Guert looked, trying not to seem to look, for the shabby schoolmaster was very near them. He walked unconcernedly nearer, staring at the wharf and at the sloop that waited there. Then, as he passed the group of three, he almost jostled Guert, and walked on with only the words, low spoken:

"It's all there. Hide it quick! I'm in danger. Don't speak!"

Guert's fingers closed upon something thin and light that he slipped into his bosom, while Up-na-tan and Co-co gazed after the schoolmaster with faces full of admiration.

"Heap chief!" muttered the Manhattan. "Fool all lobster. Heap brave" —

Just then the expression of his face suddenly changed.

Hale had reached a group of people of all sorts, outside of the guard-line at the wharf, and, as he did so, a shrill, woman's voice exclaimed:

"If that there isn't my cousin, Nathan Hale! He's a captain in the rebel army. Don't you remember, Nathan, I told you you'd be took for treason, some day? They can jest lock ye up."

"You have kept your threat, Aunt Sapphira," exclaimed Hale.

"Arrest him!" shouted the officer of the guard. "He's a Yankee spy. There's a rope waiting for him."

"Why, they wouldn't hang him?" said the woman who had betrayed him. "I thought they'd only shut him up."

"Hang him?" said the officer. "If he isn't hung or shot before sunset, he will be to-morrow."

"Then his blood is on my head!" all but screamed the woman, and she seemed to stagger as she walked away.

"Stop her!" commanded the officer.

"You don't need her," calmly remarked his prisoner. "I am Captain Nathan Hale, of Knowlton's Connecticut regiment. I'm a prisoner of war."

Guert could hear no more, for Co-co was pulling him away, and they were following Up-na-tan.

"They look like two tigers," was the next thought in Guert's mind, but they were silent until they had hurried him along for some distance. Then Up-na-tan turned his ferocious face and said:

"Guert got paper? Great chief want 'em. Hurt king men. Go! Take 'em! Tell chief Hale die" —

"Dey'll hang 'im, suah!" said Co-co. "Nebber see him again. Gone dead!"

Guert shuddered all over, but he replied:

"I'm afraid they will. Wish that woman was dead. I've got all the papers. They'll get to General Washington right away. What'll you do?"

"Ugh!" hissed rather than growled the red man. "Wait. See what do! Make 'em think Indian own island. Go! So, so, Up-na-tan!"

There was no misunderstanding his meaning. He and Co-co gave up Captain Hale as beyond hope and were already only thinking of revenge.

For one moment Guert stood still, after they left him. He shuddered from head to foot with the awful thought that his bright, heroic friend had actually given away his life.

"And I can't do one thing," he thought. "Yes, I can! I can get these papers to General Washington. I can obey Captain Hale."

It was strange to find how clear his mind became in an instant, and with what a courageous feeling he set out to do his duty, just as Hale would have done. He noticed that a very strong south wind was blowing. It was almost a gale, and it made it cooler for him to walk as fast as he did on his way to Mrs. Murray's house. He was just saying to himself:

"I'll go and tell Rachel, too," when he saw the tall, dignified form of the Quakeress going up the Murray carriage-way, and in three minutes more he was with her and Mrs. Murray and Maud in the little reading-room at the right of the hall.

They heard him with white faces, as he told of the spy-work and the capture of Nathan Hale, but when he exclaimed: "I can't get through the lines in time! They would stop me. How can I tell General Washington?" he was interrupted by Maud Walcott, and it flashed across his mind, while she spoke, "How brave she looks!"

"Aunt Wolcott," said Maud, "may I take the pony? I can carry the papers to Washington. You can send my trunk to Litchfield without me. Give them to me, Guert."

"Thee can," said Rachel. "I believe thee can do what a man could not do. Sarah, thee must let her go."

"What would her mother have said, if she were alive?" hesitated Mrs. Murray.

"She'd be just like Aunt Wolcott or Uncle Oliver," replied Maud. "They'd let me go, in a minute" — and without another word she was off after the pony.

"They may be looking out for spies to-day. Thee will hide thee at my house," said Rachel to Guert.

"Thee will know by to-morrow, what they are going to do with thy brave friend."

Guert was glad enough to remain in the city. Still, it seemed hard to surrender his precious papers to a mere girl and see her take his place as a spy. She came back leading the pony, and Rachel and Mrs. Murray helped her hide the dangerous dispatches and to mount. While they did so, Guert became aware of something more and more peculiar in the smell of the wind from the south. It did not seem warmer, exactly, but he said:

"It smells like something burning."

He could hardly speak to Maud when she cantered away, and they all stood looking after her. Mrs. Murray was crying, but Rachel was not when Guert exclaimed:

"There's a big fire in the city. I can see the smoke. I wish I could go and see what it is."

"Thee had better not," said Rachel. "Go and hide thyself at my house. Thee is a spy."

The lower wards of New York were not a pleasant place to be in, at that hour. The greater part of the houses, of all kinds, had been deserted by their former residents, and were now used as quarters for British soldiers and for army storage purposes. They were, therefore, of great use and value to the king's troops.

All the remaining people, however, and all the soldiers, were now driven out into the streets, and there were scenes everywhere, of terrible confusion and riot, for the soldiers were furious and laid upon the people, or upon Washington and his spies, the blame of a great disaster which had suddenly fallen.

Away down near Whitehall — somebody said it was near old Mom Van Boom's Shark's-Head tavern, that the Hessians had taken away from her that morning — a fire broke out, to be blown into quick fierceness by the southern gale.

Co-co and Up-na-tan were out on the beach near Hunt's shipyard when the flames burst through the roof of the barn behind Mom Van Boom's, and when they saw it they had no need to give any alarm, for anybody else could see.

"Ugh!" said the Indian. "Heap fire! Burn town. Burn lobster. Burn king gun, powder, tent, wagon, barrel. So, so, Up-na-tan!"

Co-co could hardly express the delight with which he looked at that blaze and saw how swiftly it spread among the dry, wooden buildings, but it was not many minutes before he uttered a wild yell of exultation that was followed by a whoop from Up-na-tan.

"Yo, yo! Heap o' powder went den," said Co-co. "Dah was barr'ls ob it."

Nobody knew how many barrels of powder and boxes of cartridges made up the explosion at Gaunt's warehouse, and the fire swept on with a great roar that sounded like a howl of triumph.

All over the island, even along the perpetual skirmish line between the two armies, men were thinking of that fire and were watching the dense clouds of eddying smoke. Nobody was prepared to pay much attention to a very well-dressed young lady who went cantering along as if she were out for exercise.

It was true that she went by the most unfrequented ways, and that she went rapidly, but some sentry or picket might have halted her, if it had not been for the fire.

"Redcoats!" she said, again and again. "I've seen nothing but red, so far."

There were woods on either side of a lane she at last rode into, but there seemed to be fields beyond it and then higher, broken ground.

"I know I'm near the lines," thought Maud. "Now for a run. O, pony! if you'll only run."

Down came her whip, as she dashed out at the end of the lane, just when a voice among the trees shouted:

"Halt! Stop that woman!"

"Hurrah!" replied Maud excitedly, and the pony sprang away, while the air was suddenly full of the rattle of musketry.

Probably no soldier was actually shooting at Maud, but if any meant to frighten her into halting they failed badly.

"Faster, faster!" she cried again. "Those men are in buff and blue."

The rattle ceased, and in a minute more the pony halted of his own accord, panting, but seeming satisfied, among a group of tall riflemen from whom a bronzed young fellow stepped politely forward and said :

"Lieutenant Monroe, of Colonel Mercer's Virginia Regiment" —

"Dispatches for General Washington from Nathan Hale," responded Maud breathlessly. "Quick! They have captured him and they will hang him" — her voice failed her there, and she hardly knew what answer Lieutenant Monroe made, as he took the dispatches. She only knew that he led the pony along and that very shortly she found herself under the care of Mrs. Israel Putnam and felt safe, and that Nathan Hale's costly dispatches had gone to General Washington.

She had done her duty, and she was very glad of it. The ladies and the officers praised her, too, but they all seemed to feel dreadfully about the news she brought of Hale's capture. The worst of it was that they could do nothing to help him.

It would have been a great relief to Guert's feelings if there had been anything more for him to do that day. As it was, he could only wait and think and watch the clouds of smoke, and wonder if Up-na-tan or Co-co had been caught, for he had not any doubt whatever about the kindling of that fire.

Others came and went, to and from the city, and before night it was known by everybody that the lower wards were in ashes up to Trinity Church. That, too, was gone, and all the buildings west of it, to the North River shore.

There had been a terrible time of violence, also, and dark stories were told, but it seemed to Guert that the darkest was brought to him, in Rachel Tarns's barn, at about sunset.

"To-morrow?" he said. "Hale is to be hung to-morrow morning?"

"Suah!" said Co-co. "Ole Beekman orchard. Co-co be dah."

"So will I," groaned Guert.

"Den Up-na-tan say he Kidd man again. Go to *Noank.*"

Co-co did not stay to talk, but Guert carried the news to the house. Nobody there felt like talking, and, when night came, Guert did not feel like sleeping. He knew there had been a military trial, and that Hale had been condemned as a spy, according to the laws of war. He felt sure, too, although he had not been there, how bravely his hero had behaved before his military judges. He could not help thinking of him, however, alone, shut up, during the long hours of that last night, with such a morning to come.

When it came, it found Guert already on his way toward the Beekman place. He knew that it was the headquarters of General Howe, and that it would be strongly guarded, but he thought:

"I'd risk anything to see him again. I'll try and tell him the papers went to Washington. If Maud had been stopped we'd have heard of it. I know she got through the lines."

Mrs. Murray already knew it, through a British officer who reported Maud's dash across the skirmish line; and she and Rachel and Mrs. Ten Eyck were feeling better that morning, except when they thought about Captain Hale.

"That's the orchard," said Guert, as he walked reluctantly near it. "There are guards enough, but they are letting everybody come. They won't stop me."

Of course not, for the British commander intended this punishment of a Yankee spy to serve as a salutary warning, and it was therefore to be public. The Beekman orchard was large and old and had not been very carefully kept. Near the road stood a tall, withered stem that sent out on one side a skeleton arm at a height of many feet from the ground. Under it was something made by carpenters and over the dead limb dangled a rope. It was around this tree that the provost-marshal's guard was posted, and there were both infantry and cavalry in the orchard, but any kind of people were permitted to throng the road and be impressed with the lesson of what would be the fate of spies.

"As near as I can," thought Guert. "There they come!"

"Ugh!" sounded behind him. "See brave!"

"Dah's de capt'n," hissed another voice, but Guert did not turn his head.

He was looking at an erect, fearless, firm-stepping form, that marched on toward the tree, between files of soldiers, preceded by a drummer beating time and followed by several officers.

They halted, and a pair of bright blue eyes met those of Guert inquiringly. Guert felt a keen sense of reward as he saw Hale's face flush with an expression of relief.

"He understands me! He knows that the papers got to General Washington," thought Guert. "Must he die, now?"

There was no haste in the way the work was doing, but there had been no pause, no hesitation, and at that moment a man was lifting the noosed end of the rope toward the prisoner, and another was folding a handkerchief.

"They have tied his hands behind him," almost sobbed Guert, but at that moment, out rang the voice of the doomed man. It was clear and steady and trumpet-like:

"I only regret that I have but one life to lose for my country."

Guert's very heart thrilled as he heard, and then it

almost ceased beating and he turned away his head. He did not look again. He was pushing his way through the crowd when he heard a loud tap of the drum, and then a groaning cry of many voices all around him. Among them all he could distinguish one that sounded like a smothered war-whoop and another that was tigerish. "It is all over now," he thought. "I will go home."

The vapor clouds from the smouldering ruins of the city came drifting around Guert, as he hurried along. He felt as if he were walking through the deepest kind of cloud until he stood in the Tarns sitting-room with half a dozen women around him, and told them the story of the death of Nathan Hale.

"Up-na-tan and Co-co," he said, "have gone to join Skipper Avery, in the *Noank*."

"Thee must serve thy country, Guert," began Rachel, but Mrs. Ten Eyck interrupted her with:

"Yes; you'll have to go, now, Guert. I have decided to stay where I am. Rachel and Sarah think we can do something for the prisoners. I'm so glad Maud will be sent home to Litchfield. Poor Captain Hale!"

"He did not feel so, mother," exclaimed Guert. "If you'd seen his face!"

"Guert," said Rachel Tarns, "thy brave friend is not dead. I will tell thee a thing. Thee is going to have a country to live for, and so long as the country lives it will count Nathan Hale the best soldier in its army. Do thee now go thy way, Guert, and stand in his place."

"Mother!" shouted Guert. "I'm old enough. I'm going now. I'm a soldier in General Washington's army — with Nathan Hale."

www.ingramcontent.com/pod-product-compliance
Lightning Source LLC
Chambersburg PA
CBHW020355030726
47496CB00007B/2156

9783337194420